Shadows of the Unknown
A Second Collection of Sinister Stories

By

Matthew Dewey

This is a work of fiction. Similarities to real people, places, or events are entirely coincidental.

SHADOWS OF THE UNKNOWN: A SECOND COLLECTION OF SINISTER STORIES

First edition. August 21, 2023.

ISBN: 979-8223178842

Written by Matthew Dewey.

Introduction

One thing I learned after years of writing is that even if you write something that scares you, it doesn't mean it will scare the next person. Some things we fear more than others, some things we don't.

However, there are some things we are all <u>scared</u> of, some things that I try to put in all my stories.

I hope you enjoy this second collection of scary stories. If you enjoy these works, I have more books available on my Patreon. Be sure to check out the first book, which is free forever!

And if you want more thrills and chills, check out my channel, The AURORA Files.

Happy sleepless nights!
Matthew Dewey

The Town of Masks

Off the beaten path is a road winding around a hill, across a plain, and through a forest, ending in a small town. A town of old buildings and no history. A town of quiet, sinister madness. A town where people wear masks and become their true selves, free of the pressure that is normally restricting their spirit. It is unfortunate that the true self of many men, if not every man, is evil in the full sense of the word.

Stanley Baker is one of the unlucky few who took a wrong turn there with his two friends, Harvey and Ethan. With a bad sense of direction and poor map reading, it is easy for a group to end up in all sorts of places. Stanley read the sign for the town, noticing there was no name, only four words.

Here, you are free.

Stanley Baker thought of those words as the buildings flanked the sides of the car, feeling anything but free. It was when they slowed to a stop in the town that they realized their mistake.

Harvey and Ethan argued with each other while Stanley surveyed the town. The buildings weren't in the best condition and without signs of movement, the town seemed to be abandoned. Stanley opened the door and stepped out onto the road, exploring the town with the others, under the watch of many unseen eyes.

It was then Stanely saw the flickering of light that he approached one building, looking through the window towards a tv screen in a dim living room. It seemed to be playing a still picture of a man in a chair, the lines on the screen indicating the age of the tape. Stanley was so focused on the video, he didn't notice the man in the room until he waved at the peeping traveler.

Stanley was frozen in place.

The man that stood in the corner of the room wore a pastel shirt, tie and pressed trousers, and smart shoes. Yet, his unruly, elbow-length hair, perfectly framed the disturbing mask he wore. It was a rabbit mask, scratched and aged. As the man walked towards the window, Stanley walked backward. He saw the dirt, the grunge, and the stains that covered the shirt and trousers.

Worst of all, Stanely saw how the mask was set in the man's face. Flesh covered the edges, overlapping. It was as if the man had never taken the mask off for many years and he simply grew around it. These conclusions were not cut off, even when the masked man closed the curtains sharply. Stanley turned to walk back to the car when he ran straight into another masked stranger, this time a woman with a skull mask.

Stanley stumbled, falling at her feet. He shook a little as he pushed himself up, shocked when the woman helped him up. She didn't say anything, she only stared at him for a moment and walked on, going about her business. Stanley jogged back to the car, finding only Harvey in the front seat with his cell phone.

Stanley could see he was filming all the masked people coming out of their homes and walking around. The people bought papers from sellers, drove old cars, and did everything anyone else would, but there were subtle differences. Nobody spoke, they only stared at each other. Whatever meaning they conveyed, seemed to be understood, as some would part happily while others would storm off.

Harvey began to describe one scene he saw to Stanley, but Stanley stopped him with a question. Where was Ethan?

Unable to provide a real answer, the two left the car in search of their friend. Keeping their distance from the masked ones, the travelers soon found themselves walking the length of the small town, past the old stores and buildings, without a sign of their friend. It was only out of pure desperation that one suggested they ask one of the townsfolk.

Stanley approached the most normal-looking person they could find and asked him if they had seen their friend. The man stared at Stanley, his eyes unblinking behind a disfigured mask. With their patience running thin, the two almost walked away, but then the masked man pointed at a street. With nothing else to go on, Harvey and Stanley marched onwards, growing more uncomfortable by the minute.

Harvey remarked on how naked he felt not wearing a mask in such a town. Stanley agreed but kept that information to himself.

Further down the indicated road, Harvey heard a scuffle between two buildings. He turned to see Ethan running out from the shadows, his clothing cut and blood beginning to stain. Harvey approached his friend to help but immediately froze as he saw the masked men behind him with knives.

Ethan stumbled between Stanley and Harvey, looking back at his assailants. The masked men didn't stop, their bloody kitchen knives at the ready to finish what they started. The three friends didn't stay to fight, they simply ran for their car. It was only when they turned down the road they parked their car on did they realize it had been moved.

With no car in sight, the three were half-tempted to run to the next town.

Looking back, they saw the masked men with knives still walking towards them, while the other masked people didn't seem to notice or care. Finding the fight within himself, Harvey decided to confront the two masked men, his attacks effective. Knocking one to the ground, Harvey then focused on the second. Finding their courage, Ethan and Stanley joined Harvey.

After disarming one, Harvey was caught by surprise as the other drove a knife into his shoulder. The pain only urged Harvey to act more aggressively, eventually wrenching the mask painfully from the assailant.

Behind the mask was a face beyond the imagination of the three travelers. Having only slits for nostrils and a mouth which was crossed with stitches of flesh, as if the lips were growing into each other, the unmasked man started with horror. He was not scared of the three travelers, but of the rest of the masked people as they seemed to home in on him.

The three friends backed away from the man as the whole town surrounded him as he writhed on the ground. His pale, underdeveloped face he tried to cover with the mask, but it kept falling off. More townspeople surrounded the unmasked one and a silent signal triggered them all. It was like piranhas swarming a piece of bloody meat.

The masked townspeople attacked the man. Unable to see beyond the backs of the people, the travelers had only the screams to understand the unspeakable things the masked ones did to him. In that burning light of day, with not much reason to stay, the three friends jogged towards the town exit. It was there they found their car, parked at the very edge.

Standing by their car was the woman with the skull mask. The three friends didn't approach her. Ethan was badly injured and Harvey was worse off. The woman in the skull mask through the car keys towards Ethan, who caught them gratefully. Harvey and Ethan climbed into the car, still keeping their distance from the masked woman. Ethan smiled as the engine revved to life.

Stanley approached the car, but the masked woman stepped between him and the door. The masked woman seemed to sense something from Stanley and she clutched his wrist. Stanley pulled away only for a moment but stopped when she placed a mask in his hand. He stared down, understanding. The masked woman walked back towards town, stopping at the edge, waiting for him.

Stanley Baker looked back at the town, reading the sign once more.

Here, you are free.

The Second Anomaly

The Horizon Mission was the first mission of its kind and as such, it had its risks. It required reaching new worlds, finding interesting samples, and perhaps answering questions we had about the universe. The risks were mainly financial, rather than technological. We had no problem sending astronauts up and on their way, just problems keeping the station going for many years. The solution was to cut costs and keep a single, low-paid employee; me.

I entered the station every day for nine years, waiting for a message to be received. It was around this time that the astronauts were expected to have crossed several solar systems, wake up, and land on the nearest planet with a hospitable atmosphere. Of course, we have no way of knowing this until they send us...me...a message.

The only signal I had to go on was the annual signal their ship sent me once a year.

A signal that in the last two years I hoped would never arrive. After all, I had given so much of my life for this expedition. No amount of meaningless hobbies could make up for such lost time. It's the eighties for god sake, I deserve a life just like everyone else!

At least, that's what I told myself in the tense moments. That I might as well abandon it, give the job to someone else, or close operations. I could pretend I never received the signal, thus ending the Horizon mission on a disappointing note, but ending it nonetheless. Of course, I'm an emotional sucker and could never do that.

Each year I receive the 'OK' signal from the ship I feel an incredible sense of wonder. That out there, light years away, there is a lone metal craft with a group of brave explorers. That to them, only a few months have passed, not nine years. I'd give anything to see what they were seeing when they woke up. The beauty of endless, unexplored space.

Of course, I was given my opportunity, just not in the way I expected.

March 15th, 1986, the broadcast was received. My day had just about ended and I was going to return home. The video began. Footage of the inside of the Horizon played. A shaky camera was lifted from a table by a recognizable figure. All this information came so suddenly, I found myself clinging to one of the many empty desks.

The footage was of the first astronaut awake, Dr David Browning. Unchanged by time, he still had frozen water hanging off his face. He related his feelings. He described how little feeling he had in his body at that moment, how everything was slowly waking up. As he spoke, the second and third astronauts awoke. Robert and Morgan Taylor, brother, and sister, wrenched their cold bodies from the pods they had been sleeping in.

I was already in tears when I saw Browning, but seeing the Taylor twins had me weeping.

I started making calls as I watched the video, contacting the old team and then the officials, who in turn contacted the investors and the media. It was front-page news across the world, the Horizon mission had progressed, and the astronauts were awake. Funding poured in as new investors joined the old. Non-believers became believers as the Horizon starship had proven that interstellar travel was now possible.

I was no longer alone. Joined by many of my old colleagues, who embraced me with incredible joy, I felt newfound energy within me. I never left the station, I didn't sleep. I continued to watch the footage from the moment it started and much like the cinema, more and more people entered to join me. We watched as all fifteen astronauts rose from their pods, laughing and warming up in the starship.

There were only four of us in the station. We continued to watch the broadcast, although now we watched it in shifts. Pieces of the broadcast were shared on the news to verify our claims, and a few days later it got its channel. The world was watching with me.

Watching it all unravel.

First, Browning had started a second broadcast, a camera focused on one of the windows of the ship. We could watch the stars pass by, intrigued by the clusters of light. Browning explained the readings he was receiving, on how the ship was doing as well as the health of the astronauts. A necessary second channel for us in the station to follow.

However, it ended up just being me, as everyone was more interested in the interactions and discoveries of the main crew. Browning provided ample information, but what intrigued me was the view of space. A visible distortion in the stars.

There was no point in pointing it out to Browning, as he would only receive the message a year from when I sent it. Confirmation of receiving their broadcast is the only signal we can send their ship with any sense. We, the ground control, the heads of the operation, were stuck with the role of observer and nothing else.

Still, at that moment, it was only a minor problem. Money was rolling in, upgrades were being made as a lot had changed in a decade. People were talking about us and our work in almost every home and I will admit I even got lost in the fame. A month passed before my eyes caught something else.

A conversation between the Taylor twins I overheard on Browning's camera. The twins were arguing, but before I could catch anything, Browning had silenced them. The three walked away to discuss it further. Worried, I isolated their voices and listened to a much clearer conversation.

"How long? It looks close..."

I identified it as Morgan's voice, but Browning and Robert were hard to separate.

"We don't know, it's just there."

"It has no predictable trajectory...which is worrying, as everything has a trajectory in space."

"Then what is it?"

"We think it is another ship."

Silence.

"God..."

"We need to keep this from reaching the earth. We were briefed on this, we can't let it get out."

"Why? This is huge! It's...it's groundbreaking, Bob."

"You know how people will act. Can you imagine how Johnson will act? Imagine millions of him, fueling a confused, scared, and then angry mob mentality."

"But what if it's good news? What if they are good? Can we make-"

"Please, you two, shush. We will inform the others, one by one, and keep it off-camera. If you want to discuss this further, come with me."

The voices faded, yet the camera remained fixed on the view of space. My mind was blank, I was unable to speak. I suppose I was simply trying to process the information, but at that moment I didn't think at all. I felt confused, but not confused as to what I heard and what it meant. I was emotionally confused as if I didn't know the best way to respond.

It was an anomaly.

I cut the tapes, disposing of several sections as quickly and quietly as I could. With everyone fixated on the showmanship of the rest of the crew, the wonders of space and all, I packed my suitcase and left early. Over the next week, I re-routed Browning's broadcast to my office only.

I watched the footage again. I analyzed the shape that I vaguely recognized. I compared data and received the expected results. I looked back at the door, hearing the merriment from the command center, feeling a deep sense of fear.

It was happening again.

The Grave Tender

A pleading voice called from the mortal realm. The ritualistic chant reverberated all across the great graveyard. The sickly sky and its foreboding clouds began to churn into a green and gray mass, spiraling fiercely over a single grave. All graves were open, as were their coffins, revealing the still faces within, resting in eternal slumber. The chant called for one spirit, a chosen man urged to live again.

Awakened, the chosen spirit coughed and spluttered, the taste of the sea in his mouth and lungs. His eyes were reddened by the fear his face wore in his last moments. The chosen spirit remembered the storm and the rocking ship. He remembered dying in the coldest waters, staring up at the silhouette of his ship as he sank into an inky void.

He did not wake in a void, for that would give him rest, that would give him peace.

Instead, the chosen spirit woke up in a nightmarish plain. The land was sinister and deathly, flat for the most part, yet dotted with hills with a single, lifeless tree atop each. The graves were many, the cold faces disturbing in their various forms. He alone felt the overwhelming sense of helplessness of waking up in the endless plain of the damned.

The chosen spirit heard the voices now, the chanting. Raising his eyes from the graves and their contents, he saw the yellow cracks of lighting stutter across the swirling mix of clouds. The darkness at its center appeared more welcoming than the land of the dead. It was his longing to leave the grave that fulfilled the second part of the ritual and from the clouds a bolt of lightning descended, slow and powerful.

The chosen spirit watched it gradually descend, whipping deadly tendrils that receded as quickly as they grew, till the main branch crashed into one of the small white trees nearest him. The light grew blinding until the chosen spirit could not bear to look at it. Once the light faded, the white tree called to him with voices much louder, much clearer than before, It was these voices that awoke the many dead around the tree.

Unlike the chosen, the ones that awoke were not wanted and as such, their forms reflected their twisted desire to steal from the chosen; to live again in another form.

The gray, bony forms of the ghouls climbed from their earthly resting place and fought amongst each other to reach the chanting white tree first. The chosen spirit moved towards it as well, running between the graves with the highest hopes of somehow reaching the ancient, leafless birch. His hopes began to fade as the mass of ghouls surged up the gray hill towards the tree.

Yet, the ghouls had not only each other to fear, but the Grave Tender himself.

A cloaked figure with a sinister demeanor descended like an angel of death from the darkness of the clouds. Wearing a cloak of the deepest smoke, the Grave Tender, a giant amongst the dead, fell at the foot of the tree. The force of his descent pushed all the tree's surrounding ghouls back down the hill. The gray dead tumbled, rising again to look at the colossal figure in hatred.

From the smoke, the Grave Tender's arm rose, withdrawing a black staff. The ghouls faltered at the sight of the weapon, but only for a moment before they continued their climb. The first was cut down in one sweep of the cruel instrument, their pale, shining blood coating the invisible blade of The Grave Tender's deadly instrument. One, then many at a time, were sliced to pieces, for it was not a staff, but a scythe with an invisible blade.

With each stroke, the white blood made it clear for all to see and many trembled.

The blade not only destroyed the terrible spirits but threw them back into a deep slumber, lifeless ash scattered across a lifeless land, like dead stars in an empty night sky.

The chosen spirit saw all this.

He saw all the horror, even felt the droplets of a ghoul's white blood across his skin, saw splatter across the faces of the still slumbering forms of the dead. Yet, the chosen spirit did not hesitate and he continued his sprint towards salvation. It wasn't long before he joined the waves of ghouls, only to be turned upon by the deathly figures.

Their bony forms were weak, but their claws were sharp. Although the chosen spirit could wrench his body from its grasp, it paid a price in pain. A coldness unlike any other surged through him with every scratch, with every cut. Yet, the chosen spirit continued onward, his form not slowed by pain, but instead, motivated by it. Voices that he heard so clearly amongst the bony chattering of the ghouls, so clearly amongst the song which the Grave Tender's scythe sang with every sweep.

Although the words of the chant did not mean to encourage him, only guide him, the chosen spirit found a deep desire in them. A desire greater than any of the ghouls around him, and their attempts to stop or slow him were futile. Even as his heart screamed in horror at the sight of their foul figures, it never gave in, not for a moment.

The chosen spirit battled his way through the ranks of the undead, until he too was at the foot of the hill, standing amongst the thousands of broken corpses. Some of these pieces pitifully tried to climb the hill, dying in the shimmering smoke that washed down the hill from the menacing Grave Tender.

The chosen spirit stared up at the cloaked figure of Death, into the shade of its hood and the darkness stared back. The Grave Tender raised the scythe, singling the chosen spirit out from the rest of the dead, and brought its scythe down. Unlike the mindless ghouls, the chosen spirit moved out of the scythe's deadly arc and continued his climb.

Behind the chosen spirit, the ghouls followed. The Grave Tender returned to its wide, deadly arcs, which cut through the ghouls with ease. Yet, the chosen spirit only fell flat against the hill, the scythe sweeping over him, cutting the odd, dried grass ahead of him like the odd hairs on the back of his head. The chosen spirit was on his feet in a moment and continued to climb, leaping above the sweeps, or narrowly avoiding them by falling flat to the ground.

The Grave Tender was unfazed, continuing its onslaught, killing many ghouls when it did not kill the chosen spirit.

In the end, the Grave Tender could not stop the chosen spirit. The spirit ran through the smoke of its cloak towards the white tree. The chosen reached the tree, which splintered as he neared, splitting open into a cruel arch. Without thinking, the chosen ran through the arch.

Now, he only heard voices, voices that chanted strange words.

The voices surrounded him, manifesting into an unclear image of another world. A world of the living, although his eyes could not make them out properly. It was as if he were looking through frosted glass and what appeared to be lights could have been shadows, making the world seem more unusual than it should have been. The chosen spirit found himself unable to move as if he were fixed onto a wall, unable to move his arms, legs, or head. He could only listen and watch as life slowly returned to him.

What the chosen spirit heard next was a single voice calling to him, a voice that felt so familiar. A name circled his mind but never registered. It was a voice he had known for so long, but could not remember. Yet, he felt that he soon would, that it all would become so familiar. It gave him hope, a sense of hope that made his heart feel warmer with each second.

A sound echoed behind him.

A sound that should not be, yet, was.

A sound familiar, singing.

More familiar than the voice.

The chosen spirit recognized it. The sound of the Grave Tender's scythe, slicing through the air. It was a disheartening sound that grew louder with every passing second as the Grave Tender approached.

Although it did not speak, the Grave Tender's intentions were more than clear, as it conveyed its purpose to the chosen spirit.

It was not meant to punish but to save. To prevent crimes against life and death, to ensure their balance. The Grave Tender's purpose was not evil, yet, it was not good either. It was a purpose that needed to be fulfilled, that would be fulfilled. There were no desires, no obstacles, nothing holding it back. Nothing could hold it back.

Although he could not see it, the chosen spirit could feel the blade of the scythe pass behind his neck. Cutting closer, until it graced the skin on the back of his neck and again, deeper. On the third stroke, the kiss of the blade was enough to draw blood, but the chosen spirit did not die.

***

The chosen spirit awoke.

There were three cultists around him. One, a woman, stepped towards the altar and tears welled up in her eyes. The chosen spirit looked back at her and she broke, falling over his chest and weeping into his shirt. That sense of familiarity returned. The weeping, the voice, it was his daughter. He raised his aged hand and placed it on her shoulder. The cultists had fished him from the water during the storm and upon reaching home, began the forbidden ritual.

All to save him, to bring him back, and lead them again.

The chosen spirit relished the moment. His body slowly regained its strength, his senses returning to him. Each breath was deeper than the last, as he drank fresh air again. With excitement, the chosen spirit placed his hands on the altar he laid upon and tried to sit up.

As he did, he felt a pain unlike any other, causing him to sit up in an instant. It wasn't the effort that made him feel that way, but his neck. He grunted the word 'neck', causing the others to examine him more closely. The cultists could see a small cut, as thin as paper, yet, from the cut a single drop of gray blood formed, finally falling onto the altar.

All four examined the curious droplet, only to watch it shift into smoke and then grow into a cloud of gray. The cloud grew to surround them as if they were caught in an ocean of mist. From the smoke grew a large figure, skeletal at first. The haunting figure was familiar to the chosen spirit and then all his memory returned as the Grave Tender stood in the mortal realm before him.

All four stood, surrounding the Grave Tender, feeling a fear that froze them in place.

The Grave Tender examined the three figures that began the ritual. Without love, without hatred, the Grave Tender swung his scythe. The cultists were split, destroyed, broken into red ash, and their remains joined the forceful spiral of smoke, turning it from gray into a terrible crimson.

Surrounded by the red of his cult, of his family, the chosen spirit finally broke.

The Red Death stood before him, a figure of cruelty, of punishment. Without mercy, it had destroyed those closest to the chosen spirit. Even though he had only returned to the mortal world for just a moment, the chosen spirit wished to return to the open grave he slept in.

However, as his humanity returned to him, so did his lust for power. Witnessing the might of the Red Death only served to inspire the chosen spirit to cling to life a little longer.

As the Red Death raised the scythe, the chosen spirit fell to his knees and tried to bargain. He pleaded for power and in return, he would pay with the blood of all his followers. The Red Death did pause, it did hesitate, but not to consider the offer, but to punish the chosen spirit in a way it felt most fitting.

The chosen spirit felt the Red Death's meaning, the unspoken words, once more. He knew then that there was no hope for him or his following.

The Red Death walked amongst the mortals, amongst the innocent and the guilty. With incredible power, the Red Death would destroy all that the chosen spirit created and he would live only to watch it happen before the Red Death removed him from existence. For he was only the Grave Tender in the land of the dead, but in the mortal realm, he was a cruel and angry god.

The chosen spirit would suffer a punishment greater than any other.

To be erased from all time, from the past, present, and future. All his influence, all those memories, to be struck from the record of the universe and then instead of being scattered across the graves, the chosen spirit would be thrown into oblivion.

The chosen spirit saw all this and the Red Death willed it into being. Once done, it returned to the land of death, to tend to the graves of the damned, to fulfill a purpose.

Don't Open the Door

The nights I spent in front of the fireplace, pondering the sounds from the street, were unnerving, to say the least. The warmth of the fire could not stop the shiver running down my spine as the sound echoed down the stone street. Akin to a creak of a door opened so slowly, the sound erupted from what sounded humanoid, shaking me to my core. Every night it grew closer and closer until the pained groan was outside my very door.

I would stare with wide, fearful eyes at my door. The sound penetrated it better than any blade, filling my ears with its agony. Even the room felt darker, the fire seemed to die almost to its last embers before the creature would pass completely. As the sound faded, warmth returned, but peace did not. I would find myself stuck in a trance, pondering the sound more, unable to stop myself. It was only when my body begged for sleep, or the fire popped loudly, that I would wake up.

I never armed myself, as I didn't see the need.

Sounds do not cut the flesh. There were no marks on my door when I checked in the morning, and no evidence to prove what I was hearing was even real. Be it my wild imagination or exhaustion-induced delirium that conjured the illusion, I cannot say. Yet, I could not excuse it as some plague of the mind. In my cowardly heart, I knew that the sound was real, that creature making the sound was real.

After another terrifying night, I returned to my work the next day. A metalwork factory near the harbor, however, my work involved paper and ink. I typed out in monotony a sequence of records for the company, a glorified secretary more than a manager, although I was often called upon to solve problems in the factory itself. It was the respect of the workers that seemed to calm me by the end of the day.

Having worked with them all before on the factory floor, I knew them well and they knew me. I saw in their eyes the concern of friends, although I knew they would not admit it to save me pride. Instead, they showed it through not-so-subtle questioning and invites to the pub. Drinking did not have the same effect on me as it did on them and as such, I always refused, choosing to stay home and lock my doors before night fell.

That is what gave me comfort.

A column of deadbolts secured the only entrance to my home. I lived on a quiet street, many houses packed against each other. I thought that if the day did come when the creature that wandered the streets decided to invade a home, that mine would withstand its attempts of forced entry. That it would stalk down the street, setting its sinister sights on some other home. That I would be spared the cruelty in its heart, that I would escape its terror, somehow, for good.

Yet, my deadbolts were never tested.

Every night it came and passed, but despite the predictable routine, I never felt secure. I always felt that it would eventually break through the door, in a horrific display of power, that I would be spotted, defenseless. I could imagine the shadowy figure of some colossal monster charging me from the doorway, that I would not have time to even scream.

Thoughts such as these never seemed to leave me. Incessant corruption spread itself throughout my mind, of death and suffering. Yet, despite the thoughts never ceasing, my crumbling mind began to ponder not only the sound but the appearance of the creature. Was it human? Perhaps it was a dog, abused and damaged? Did it harbor any dark intentions, as I so believed?

Although my fears never dwindled, my curiosity surely grew. It was curiosity that made me so vulnerable. A morbid interest in what was beyond the shadows of the night, what hunted in the darkness rather than slumbered. It was curiosity that drove me to move from the warmth of my fireplace, sitting near the window beside my door. Through a gap in the curtains, I watched the street lights flicker to life, the last horses and carriages rove on by.

I saw the stars and the moon radiate in the night sky and found myself calmed by their sight. It had been so long since I had seen anything of the night having chosen to stare only at the back of my door or dancing flames below my mantle. My peace was short, as clouds moved to block the sky from sight. Light poured through the clouds only enough for me to make out the silhouettes of the buildings, it was now only the streetlights that revealed the secrets of the shadows.

With each passing minute, my anxiety grew, unsettled by the silence as lights within homes flickered out until all buildings were dark. For a moment, I felt like retreating to the fire, or better, to the bed where I would force myself into a drug-induced slumber before I heard the nightly call.

As the thought began to gain purchase, it immediately ceased as I heard the faint creaking of the creature. Its moan echoed, but I did not see a single light flicker from any window. I did not see any reaction to the growing disturbance. I watched an unchanging street, staring down the pavement in the direction the sound was going. From my position, my left ear was on the wall and my eyes were fixed on the dirty glass.

It felt like it was approaching me from behind, the wall seeming thinner and thinner by the second. A second sound became apparent, the footsteps of the beast. Despite my growing fear, I was once more transfixed by the call, unable to move or think clearly.

I could hear the footsteps on the other side of the wall, only inches from me. My spirit drained as the figure came into view. A slumped silhouette at first, but the clouds cleared to reveal it in its full horrific glory.

Human, in some respects, but a monster in others. The body was bent, broken as if mangled like a clay doll in a child's hands. It became apparent that the creaking noise it created was one of pain, noise escaping what had to be a tortured throat. Despite the disgust and the empathy, there was no pity in my heart.

My eyes narrowed to examine the shambling creature further. It must have felt my stare, as it turned to face my front door. I could no longer feel my heart at that moment as I caught a glimpse of the man's face, for it was a man. I could make out the shape of its contorted face, but nothing else. Without a creak of its terrible voice, it examined my door in the most menacing silence.

In my gut, anger began to form. I feared this creature, I was disgusted by it, but I believed that I could fight it if the need arose. The desire to fight it grew, like a dark evil within me, but I could not help but feed it with more fear, like coal into a furnace. Yet, it did not attempt to enter, it didn't even touch the door.

That's when it leaned towards the window.

It surprised me at first, but then I saw why when its face was illuminated by a ray of moonlight breaking through the clouds; the eyes of the strange creature were on the sides of its head! It was never staring at the door, but rather straight at me through the gap in the curtains. Its yellowish orb examined me with a fishlike expression while I replied in turn with a gaping expression of my own. It started at me as if I were an answer to all its questions.

It reached towards me, pushing against the glass. It didn't seem to comprehend what it was looking at, not understanding that the glass needed to be struck for it to reach me. I watched, unable to react until the glass began to crack. It placed both its hands against the glass, pushing with all its mutant might.

"Why me?" I asked it softly, then screamed right after.

The creature didn't respond, but its eyes were staring with absolute focus. I found myself moving as more tendrils began to spread across the glass. I spun on the spot, searching the room for something to help me fight the creature, as any weapon would be better than having to touch the creature with my bare hands. I kept picking up obscure objects, such as ink vials, papers, and even a cumbersome chair which I struggled to lift off the ground, let alone swing at the monster.

Eventually, I settled on planning my escape instead. If I could not find a proper weapon or find it in myself to fight with my hands, I would escape and find someone who would fight on my behalf.

The window shattered, and glass poured onto the floor. The creature's pained groans were louder than ever, as glass tore at its pale flesh. Despite its wounds, it continued to climb through the window, sustaining more injuries in the process. It didn't falter, only screamed louder and louder. Its pained screams filled me as they filled the room.

I shook on the spot before rushing to the door. I began undoing the deadbolts, but I was only halfway through before the creature fell onto the floor inside. I didn't continue unlocking the door, choosing to flee upstairs to my bedroom. Once there, I closed the door just in time to see its face appear at the foot of the stairs.

I had no locks to save me in my room, so I simply braced my body against the door in the hopes that it would be enough to turn away the mindless monster and its murderous might. I felt the pressure against the door, I could hear its odd breathing and grunts as it pushed in small bursts. Gradually its effort grew, along with my exhaustion.

I felt alone, delirious, and scared. It was different when it was outside, but now my anger was only replaced with cowardice. I begged it to leave, pleaded for peace, and bargained with all I had, but it showed no interest. It didn't speak a single word, only acted on instinct and aggression, which worryingly worked in its favor.

With my options fast running out, I saw only one.

I had a single, open window in my bedroom. A window that welcomed cool night air to soothe me on hot nights, but now offered me an easy escape from evil. With adrenaline fuelling my being and irrational thought, I turned to face the window. I moved from the door, dashing and then diving with little grace through the aperture.

The street did not greet me in my descent, as I expected it to. A passing carriage in the dead of night, as luck would have it, caught me. Although my fall was less than painless, I was glad that it wasn't worse.

I bid the cloaked driver continue his journey, for I was being pursued by a madman, to which he whipped the reins and the horses hastened.

Pathetically, I crawled from the top of the carriage onto the bench alongside the driver, who looked at me fearfully, asking many questions, as did the passengers in the carriage. While I answered them to the best of my ability, I was far too distracted to speak coherently, looking back at my street and home. There was no figure in sight, so I requested the driver halt at the end of the street.

I climbed down from the carriage, as did the driver, and a portly man my age climbed out of the carriage. Together, we were braver and approached my home, our voices became whispers before falling silent completely.

My home was searched, but there was nothing. Evidence of intrusion was clear, bloodstains too, but no crumpled creep and his contorted face. We were alone. I didn't want to stay alone, but the driver had his passenger to attend to, so instead, I joined them, only leaving the carriage as we approached the police station.

I filed a report.

I fixed the window, boarding it up and ensuring no further break-ins.

I didn't hear the creaking call of the creature again.

Yet, having never seen him leave my home, I wonder, fearfully, if he didn't find somewhere in my home to hide. I wonder if he has such power, to stow himself away in the smallest corner, under or within any object, away from sight. If that be the case, then I have trapped myself in a prison of my own making, while I suffer in a prison of pure, mental terror.

May Death find me in my sleep and save me from further suffering.

The Last One

There were many moments when I felt myself slipping as a human. Yet, I could hardly tell with nobody to compare myself to. Being the last of anything is a heavy feeling of sadness and futility. Somewhere, in the depths of every human being, is the desire to live on, if not as yourself, then through someone else. It could be a son, a daughter, or simply a friend you know will still be around when you are gone.

My name is Devin McLoughlin and I am the last one.

I found myself swaying between the decision to persist or to end it. It would have been an easier choice for me to leap from the large structure to the hard metal below, but somehow I didn't. I found myself mentally defending the option to live on. I told myself that there was hope, that there were others. I just couldn't find them. Yet, in my heart, I knew the answer.

My existential journey began when I was sent into space. A space station was built, larger than any other and unfortunately smarter than anything. When Earth met its demise at the hands of this extraordinary AI, I was sleeping deeply. Despite the distance between the station and Earth, I still felt the explosion. The force was astronomical and I awoke to see it tear apart. The horror on my face was clear to see, reflected in the thick glass I stared through.

On instinct, I ran out into the station, towards the command center of the structure. I was the only one on the station purely by chance, repairing a minor problem before the real inhabitants took their place. I thought about the emptiness as I ran, questioning my sanity. Had it been an illusion, brought on by some form of cabin fever? Was I having a nightmare, worse than any other?

I was not.

Upon reaching the command center, I checked recordings in the station's log and discovered footage of the station being the direct cause. Volatile matter, contained and kept in the station's storage, had been directed towards Earth. A weapon of devastating power devised and constructed by the AI that controlled the station had been completed and tested on Earth.

It was a simple misinterpretation of Earth's orders. The AI was aware of weapon testing areas on Earth, it chose the most suitable and fired the weapon. An area in the ocean was targeted, having the largest radius available on Earth to test such a weapon. Life was exterminated, the test a success and the AI began work on other projects.

It felt like science fiction, but it wasn't a rogue AI, simply a poorly created one. The destruction of all life fell on human shoulders and I alone had that guilt to carry. Hundreds of thousands of years of dangerous curiosity led to this moment and I was left alone to take responsibility.

The nightmares that followed had a terrible effect on my psyche.

Three weeks passed after that day and I felt myself drifting. Sadness was overwhelming, and thoughts and memories seemed to fade. Almost as if my mind decided I didn't need them anymore. If that could happen in a few weeks, I worried about what would happen in a few months. Time, unstoppable, would be my demise.

Yet, I didn't feel lonely. I didn't long for human company. When I wanted to share my thoughts, simply speaking them aloud for my ears to hear was enough. Once more, I didn't realize that speaking to the air without mental stability would lead to me speaking to people who weren't there...and hearing them speak back.

***

"Where is the ...the...uh," Devin sighed to himself. "Where is the wrench? Red wrench, red, red, red, red wrench."

Devin droned to himself as his hand rummaged through the toolbox. Upon finding the wrench, he began working with the nuts and bolts to get the metal panel loose. Once done, it fell to the ground, one corner catching his foot painfully. Devin cursed, hopping one foot. His screams were loud, louder than he ever screamed in a long time.

"Right, right, that's enough, calm down, stop, stop...stop hurting!" Devin yelled again, rubbing his foot. Once he regained his composure, he knelt and moved the panel to the side, revealing a wall of pipes and electrical boxes. "A...A15, that should be...should be..."

Finding it, Devin opened the electrical box, the smell of melting wire hitting him immediately.

"Right, looks like this needs a standard insulator."

"Yes, and plenty of cooling gel," Devin replied, gathering the right tools. "You know...you know, the cooling gel is underrated. It's come so far...no further, but far enough...and...and..."

Devin trailed off again, the wires taking all his concentration. With power cut in that section, he clutched the rubber and peeled it straight off the wire, then began stripping the wire itself to reveal a twist of cables.

"Big...big expensive station," Devin continued.

"For a few million more, they could have built it to last with some proper stuff."

"My thoughts exactly. It's no wonder the AI flipped out... if it's coded as well as this station is constructed."

Devin continued to speak to nobody and nobody continued to speak back.

***

I blame myself, but there are still moments that make me think...it was something else. I found food I never found before, places that shouldn't have been there. As time went on, I found new areas in the station, lacking any human interface in all cases, yet, designed with humans in mind. It lacked all the switches, dials, and buttons, but it had doorways, and it had stairs.

I walked down empty corridors and circled empty rooms. I found fresh wiring leading to new lights, rivets still hot from the machines that inserted them into the metal plating. The station was under construction but without any human involvement. In my mind, it had to have been the AI, but without the proper permissions, it could do nothing more than control basic functions beyond the Research & Development Center.

The lights would turn off at a certain time, then turn back on at another time. It was the only way I could accurately measure the days passing by but despite that, lights, doorways, heating and cooling, small minor things compared to the construction of new wings to the station.

With that said, that still left the question unanswered. Who or what was expanding the station?

***

"I...I..." Devin stuttered. "I-it makes no s-s-s-...it makes no s-sense. T-the doors, they are too far apart, but that's just my opinion...it c-could simply be the...the design choice. Must be some designer, one of those s-sp-special d-designers, the real eccentrics, you know?"

"I know the type, never had the chance to meet one. Still, the rooms are hardly classy."

"Not at all."

"Definitely a 'no' from me."

"Me too, but I like the room sizes. Plenty of space to work in, could have tables of parts and work on several projects without any clashing with each other."

"You know, that's n-not a bad idea," Devin pointed out. "I need a new place t-t-to work. Well, the lights are still on, let's start moving stuff...everyone."

Devin looked around at the empty room with an optimistic smile and fast-walked out to collect desks from the spare rooms. Without a pang of sadness, without a feeling of emptiness, without questioning anything, David worked happily.

Three years have passed since Earth's destruction.

***

It took me a while to realize I could not depend on *them*, of course. There were very few opportunities for me to challenge their reality. Not to mention...it didn't take long for my eyes to start deceiving me as well as my ears. I saw faces, but not human faces like mine. What I saw was...it was like seeing someone familiar through frosted glass. A blur, but an arrangement of features you knew so well you could fill in what was missing.

I didn't have names for them, they didn't have names for themselves, but these people were what kept me going. I hate to think what would have become of me had madness not saved me. A sane person wouldn't have made it as far as I did or did the things I was willing to do. It's true what they say, that once you hit rock bottom, there's nowhere to go but up.

I hit rock bottom and there was nowhere for me to go, so my mind made it seem like there was. It made it feel like what I was doing was right, the way I was living, the way I was thinking. I felt happier in that overwhelming misery than I had ever felt before and I almost wanted to stay that way...but that's no way to live.

We're all just dying slowly, but that was the definition of what I was going through. A dead man walking, nothing to tell him he was alive and nothing to tell him being dead was bad.

***

A shuttle found its way to the space station, locking onto the docking bay. After an hour of technical work, one of the engineers felt it was secure enough for the doors to open. The two technologies were only made compatible with enough careful tinkering, where one mistake could have led to the death of every man and woman on the shuttle.

When the doors opened, the group of remaining humans saw the wondrous station and climbed aboard. Having seen the expansion over the past three years in the shuttle, everyone felt themselves breathing deep, having more space than they had in a long time. Despite this sudden comfort, all were shocked to see nobody else, not a soul.

Splitting into groups of four, the survivors went on a search for the other survivors on the station, but many were simply picking out their rooms and thinking of the time they would spend on the station. To them, it would be a life greater than the one they were spending on the old station, which had grown far too small for them.

One particular group approached the out-of-place doors which led to the expansion someone had created for the station. The four marveled at the design, seeing the faults, but all were superficial. As they walked, they saw tables of instruments and machines, broken and experimented with by some brilliant engineer.

That's when they found Devin, clinging to a window, staring out into space, talking to himself in angry, hushed tones.

One of the survivors took a step closer, but another held him back. Turning around, Devin saw the strange, monstrous faces and his eyes widened. In desperate fear, he grabbed the closest metal tool and held it threateningly. With great caution, the survivors approached Devin, in the hopes of bringing him back to sanity, and their hopes were almost dashed.

Hearing voices foreign to him, Devin attempted to kill himself as a means of preserving his mind and heart in their last moments. To die with knowledge of only the voices and faces he saw. Before he fainted from the loss of blood, one of the survivors came real close for Devin to study her face. Sadness returned to him so sweet and he told her as he cried, "They made me do it, they made me do it, they will kill you too. Leave...".

After waking in the medical bay, being treated by three doctors who were so glad to work with an unfamiliar patient and an unfamiliar problem, Devin tried to remember the ones who kept him company. He tried to remember the person he was before he saw real people again, but could not. Devin shook hands with many new people, people he was so happy to see.

Happy, whole people, who showed Devin so much humanity in a few minutes that he felt all his humanity rushing back. One showed their kids, another showed their simple little inventions made from spare parts, showing their admiration for his work, one showed him a mirror, with his clean-shaven face and a new haircut. Tears welled up in his eyes, as he saw a face he had not seen for so long, touching his cheeks which felt so smooth, aside from the self-inflicted cuts that would heal with time.

***

"And, do you still see *their* faces?" the doctor asked, concern on his face.

"No, I don't. I can remember them now, I can remember a lot of it, but I don't see them," I replied.

"Are you happy about that?"

"Yes, I am, more than I can describe."

"And...do you still hear them?"

Not a single one.

"Not a single one," I smiled.

Facade

Mrs. Dorian died in apartment 13F. I didn't know her, her neighbors didn't know her, nobody knew her, yet it seemed everyone who lived in the building felt a pang of sadness to see her go. When I took the apartment, I saw her being carried out. It wasn't a welcoming sight, but the people who stood in their apartment doorways made up for it. I was greeted with kindness and heartwarming compliments.

All-in-all, it was the most unusual building I had ever lived in, but I had to admire it. Everyone was quiet, considerate, and had all the best qualities of the ideal neighbors. The sweet smell of baked goods wafted from their apartments into the halls, the doors were often held for me, so I did the same for them. I never had conversations with strangers, but these people approached me, introduced themselves, and told me stories up to my floor.

Within a month, I felt like I knew them so well, better than the people I worked with.

Yet, that kindness seemed only to be a facade for something sinister. I was lured into the building's embrace, only to find it throttling while I smiled ignorantly. As time passed, I noticed that there never seemed to be a moment where they weren't smiling. Always happy, never having a bad day. It was curious, but when I saw one smiling tenant climbing the stairs with heavy shopping bags, I soon realized the gravity of my situation.

The shopping bags broke, all contents spewed down the stairs, and many were broken and poured out onto the carpet at the bottom. All that the tenant did was smile wider, to my horror, as if the pain thrilled him. Yet, I could see the resistance on his face, as if someone told him to smile at gunpoint.

Of course, being a simple-minded person, I didn't think too much of it. It was weird, but when something weird happens in your everyday life you just tell your friends about it later and move on. Unfortunately, this was what I did instead of investigating. Another month passed before I knew it and once more, I found myself acting the same way.

I was kind to my neighbors whenever I could be. I even began learning their schedules, mentally readying myself to go help my neighbor in room 13E with his dog walking, since he had more than a single dog. Such good-natured helpfulness was infectious and it had a profound effect on me. Yet, I didn't seem to notice how strange it was that I would sit by the door and listen to the soft clicks of dogs' nails on the corridor floor.

It was thanks to my friend that I noticed something was off.

I was having coffee with them one day. Upon taking my coffee from the barista, I turned without looking and bumped my friend. The coffee spilled on me, which of course, caused a lot of pain. I felt it, my emotions were raised, and I thought I was freaking out like I normally would, but I wasn't. My friend pointed this out when we left the coffee place.

According to him, I simply embraced the pain somehow. I was even smiling, but my eyes didn't seem to be smiling at all. It wasn't like I was acting tough, but more like I was afraid of showing any kind of negative emotion. Understandably, I realized the madness of it and recalled a similar experience. I thought back on that neighbor whose grocery bags broke and I was shocked to see the similarities between our stories.

You would think I would just start watching myself closely or even move to another building, but my curiosity got the better of me. I was more interested in why they acted that way, not the effect it was having on me. Not knowing where to start slowed this investigation down, but it was thanks to a conversation with one of my neighbors that I learned more.

"That old tenant, Mrs. Dorian, so unlike you," the old woman began. "Lacked the spirit. Always so glum about everything, but never mind that, how are you doing on sugar, dear?"

I tried to learn more about Mrs. Dorian in this conversation, but I was blocked from discussing it further by more pressing questions and concerns from the old woman. Her kindness was overwhelming, as always, so I found myself lost in a delightful conversation about delightful things.

However, my curiosity was undying. By the time I realized the old woman had spoken circles around me, I was in my apartment with her chocolate-chip cookie recipe. Determined, I decided to confront the other tenants on different floors, to see if they knew anything. I was wasting my time knocking on their doors to receive no response. It seemed everyone was away on holiday, or simply there weren't any tenants on the other floors.

The gravity of that fact hit me and I decided to speak to the apartment building owner, who confirmed this fact.

"Renovations," he told me simply. "Floor 13 is the only one with adequate conditions for tenants. The others don't meet regulations, so there are no tenants."

"How long have the renovations been going on?"

"Uh...long time now, I have to get back to work," he mumbled, lowering his gaze to the papers on his desk. "If there aren't any complaints, do you mind leaving me to it?"

It wasn't just his lousy lying that bothered me. Renovations on every floor, not a sound of construction, and a manager unable to tell me how long they've been going on. There were way too many holes in the story, more than I could accept. I was afraid that my stop at the manager's office would be another dead-end, so I decided to take action.

"Yes, there's a problem with my door, I'm having trouble getting into it," I told him.

"And you came to ask me about the other floors?" the manager muttered as one of his eyebrows raised. "Should have just started with that."

"I was just making polite conversation, but I do need you to deal with it now, as I am going to work now, and I left-"

"Yes, yes, I will see to it now."

The manager pulled himself up, popping a cigarette in his mouth as he left. I listened for his footsteps and when it was safe, I dived towards the filing cabinets behind him. Everything was sorted out alphabetically, which made it much easier to find Mrs Dorian. Taking the file, I hid it in my jacket and moved to the exit. As I went, I bumped into the manager, who told me the apartment door seemed to be working fine.

In a brilliant show of quick thinking, I took out my keyring, blaming the key I chose, knowing full well it wasn't the right key to the apartment. The manager rolled his eyes and pointed this out, vaguely amused. I laughed it off as I left, thanking and apologizing as I went, with a big floor-thirteen smile.

***

Reading Dorian's file, I found her emergency contact number and phoned it straight away. The woman who picked up was Dorian's sister, who was more than surprised to be talking to a stranger about her late sister. The sister told me that she often received calls from her sister telling her about all the strange happenings.

What seemed to concern Dorian most were the neighbors that were vacating the other floors, more than the unusual behavior of the floor 13 tenants. Dorian mainly remarked how she never got to say goodbye, she had no clue they were leaving. It appeared to her that they simply disappeared into the night, as she stopped seeing them during the day. Before Dorian died, her sister discussed a diagnosis from the doctor, a terrible disease. I left the conversation there without wanting to press her further on the subject.

That was enough for me to know that something was up with the other apartments and I had to find out what.

With an old trick I learned as a kid, I was able to jimmy the lock to one of the apartments and get inside. I discovered a terrible smell and an occupied noose.

I fell to the ground, disgusted and horrified. Seeing a dead woman being carried out of my apartment was different, for one she was covered and from what I could tell, simply died of old age. A rotting corpse hanging from the ceiling was something else. Revolted, I crawled out of the room, closing the door firmly behind me.

I wish I had just left there, but I checked the next apartment and the apartment after that. Slit wrists, a bathtub of blood. Next, a poisoned man lying in a pool of blood.

No more, my mind was tortured by the sight of it all. I had to leave, so I did. I returned to my apartment and started gathering my things. Overwhelmed by horror and sadness, I found myself placing stuff back, confusingly wondering where things were, and then losing all care. I felt a sadness seep inside of me, a sadness that seemed to grow stronger by the second. I couldn't smile even if I tried, I couldn't find the energy to do anything to keep me positive.

Next, I was playing with knives. I was leaning far out of a window...I was doing things that scare me now just thinking about it. The room seemed to grow darker, despite the day. I felt a presence all around me, sinister, but I wasn't scared. The only other emotion I felt aside from sadness was emptiness. An indifference, a lack of interest, a lack of joy. I found myself feeling what I can only describe as agonizing depression.

I was suffering in nothingness.

I felt hands drag me.

I felt them slap me.

I seemed to wake up from a trance, seeing one of my worried friends and the roof of an ambulance. It seemed I chose to jump from the window, but without looking, I collided with a large, bushy tree. I felt pain, but more than that, joy. That place had taken everything from me the moment I felt down, the moment I felt truly unhappy.

It seemed to relish that pain and take it further. I felt what so many lost tenants felt and learned what the tenants on floor 13 knew. The only way one could survive in that place was to force a facade or welcome cruel darkness. The darkness that fed on their misery, ravaged them in moments of emptiness and had the remains disposed of themselves.

What was there was beyond me and I didn't return.

***

"That's another," 13A laughed as she fed her cat. "Silly, silly, isn't it silly? It's amazing how much you can eat, sprinkles!"

"Yes, yes, but you know it's nothing new," 13G replied. "I find it amusing nowadays, seeing them struggle with it. Must be the youthful spirit that keeps me going!"

"Oh, more than your youthful spirit," 13B murmured. "It's your sheer wonderfulness. You did so much for him, it's a shame he didn't appreciate it when he had the chance."

The three friends smiled at each other, their eyes telling of their misery, but the rest of their being fighting the sadness. It was torturous, breaking them slowly. In those moments, they collectively felt a unique sadness before it was dashed by 13C who brought her chocolate chip cookies into the room.

"Now listen, my darlings, don't eat too many, I've got some wonderful lasagna in the oven," 13C told them. "Just a snack until the cheese is all gooey."

The three tenants looked at 13C with grateful eyes and immediately the mood lightened. Distracted once more by simple things, the tenants of floor 13 repressed the fundamental human emotions that made life meaningful.

Wearing a bitter facade, they persisted.

Breathe

The hand hit the back of my head harder than I expected. No matter how much I braced myself for the strike, it also stung painfully. If I flinched, another would follow, so I simply moved with the stroke and followed my training. Breathe in, exhale, center. Once I did that, I was ready for the verbal abuse to follow the physical.

"I am beginning to wonder if you are ready for this," the Instructor murmured simply. Somehow, those words hurt more than physical abuse. "You lack the skill that a true killer requires. I believe if you had a loaded gun to your enemy's head, you would hand him the gun and paint a target on your forehead!"

Another sharp strike. Breathe in, exhale, center.

"Do you see the target?" the Instructor asked again.

"Yes, sir," I replied on time. If said sooner, it would be cheek, if said later, I wasn't paying attention.

"Is your reticle over their ugly face?" the Instructor asked again.

"Yes, sir."

"Is the target ready, unmoving, and ripe for the picking!?" the Instructor yelled.

"Yes, s-"

"Then take the damn shot!"

I pulled the trigger. There was a brief moment, then the window broke and the head vanished in a mist of red. Even from this distance, I could still hear the screams of the target's wife.

"Excellent, now move!" the Instructor ordered.

The gun was in the bag, the ejected shell with it. Nothing was left for evidence. I threw the bag into the trunk, knowing that it wouldn't go off with its only bullet fired. The Instructor didn't believe in second chances once the first shot was fired.

I climbed into the driver's seat and the Instructor was already waiting in the passenger's seat with a blank expression. I rolled down the windows before setting off, the day was hot and humid. The Instructor placed his forearm out the window, tanning in the summer sun.

"You need to stop hesitating, but overall, you did well," the Instructor told me. "Now, how are you feeling?"

"I-" I began.

"Wrong, you are not supposed to feel," the Instructor muttered. "Every time you get asked that you should say nothing."

"I feel cold," I told him.

The Instructor cut me a sideways glance and an amused smile spread across his lips.

"I feel cold," the Instructor repeated mockingly. "That's still a feeling, you psychopath. I don't know how many times I need to say this, but apparently, it's always one more time! Wake up!"

I stopped at the intersection and waited for the lights. Something about the crossroads added to the tension, but it was gone in moments. Breathe, exhale, center.

"You have superior form, son," the Instructor continued. "Your skill, your talent for this work is there, but you are lacking the heart for it. I'm not sugarcoating it, this is a hard job and hard jobs require a heart of steel. I can't have you go soft, you understand?"

"Yes, sir."

"Cut the 'sir' crap, will ya? Just don't go blowing this after such a long time. I joined you on your first run, you did great and nobody was the wiser. Now I need you to turn it in and get your pay. It's time to lay low, but you can still do that much."

An hour's drive later and the Instructor was sweating like a pig. He wiped a dirty hand across his face. The mixture of sweat and dirt formed mud on his now-pink forearm.

"Hell of a day and man, is hell the right word or what?" the Instructor asked.

"It sure is," I replied. "We're here."

"I can see that, son. Hurry up and get your pay. The sooner we get home the better. Jesus."

I left the car and marched towards the door across the sandy ground. If there is anything that felt hot it was the wind. The humidity makes breathing difficult, but it passed when I entered the air-conditioned shack. That chill swept over me, as it always did when the cold air cooled my sweaty skin. From one discomfort to another, I walked through the cold shack towards the cellar stairs.

Standing at the top was a man wearing a brown suit. His eyelids drooped, but not enough to cover the cold, beady eyes that stared at my approaching form.

"Complications?" he asked.

"That's not for you to ask," I muttered, walking past and down the stairs.

There was another door, this one opened electronically. Of course, they were watching. By the time I reached for the handle, there was a buzz and the door opened. I believed the doorman got a kick out of making me look like a fool.

Now entering something akin to a hospital, the clean-tiled bunker of killers greeted me the same way it always did. Uncaring stairs, grating teeth, and twitching fingers. It is almost as if they were begging me to step out of line, but that was all a precaution.

I stepped to the counter that made up the center of the room and stopped in front of a thin, young man who worked the computer. He brushed his hair constantly and rubbed his eyes.

Now words were spoken, and the cards were exchanged. When that was done, the young man slid me a fairly large envelope and returned to his computer. Tapping constantly, the young man still watched me leave the way I came from the corner of his eye.

"'Bout time, let's get," the Instructor muttered. "Never liked this place, especially that weedy teenager at the counter. His father was so much better."

"How so?" I asked as we drove back onto the tarred road.

"He had a great sense of humor."

I turned down a dirt road and followed the treeline. The bushes grew thick and soon blocked the car from view entirely as we made our way down the winding path.

"You will get used to it, son," the Instructor murmured. "Just stop watching the news."

"Yes, sir."

The Nobody

"How has it been?" the handler asked.

"Let's skip that bit and get to the part where I tell you what's happening," I murmured. "I have become a part of Chen's loyal bodyguards. I'm on shaky ground there, but give it time. We will be making this deal at a meeting point that Chen and his brother decided. We will stay there until everything is sorted out, but knowing Chen, that could take some time."

"Have suspicions been raised?" the handler asked.

"Ever since joining I have been receiving raised eyebrows, but I think they've just about lowered it. That's why I'm nervous. I like knowing that they're suspicious and in this case, they either know or they don't know I'm with the cops."

"You mentioned making a friend?"

"Yeah, Chen's daughter, six years old. She is as innocent as it gets and I watch over her with another bodyguard. I think that is the reason I've stayed on so long as Chen's guard. Usually, they are kicked out or killed, but his daughter likes me."

"I see, I was hoping for someone who could help us."

"You never know. Chen and his brother, Liu, they're bringing their young daughters to this meet-up. It's clever, it keeps bullets from flying around. I think the rest of the gang would wage a war to the death over these girls."

"Have you narrowed down the meeting point?"

"Just a few places. The garage shop in Chen's front yard is ideal for us, but not for Liu. Still, ending a feud requires sacrifices and that's why I think Liu might cave in. There is also a china store, but that doesn't have any place for people to sleep, which is why I think the hotel will be ideal. There have been reports of disappearances there. It being in Liu's territory, he thinks it best the brothers work on fixing that when they're not discussing the feud."

"I know Chen is in his forties, but how old is Liu?"

"Sun Liu is pushing forty, the youngest brother."

"No respect?"

"None, probably one reason he was happy to start a feud in the first place. However, you remember their father. I think with the anniversary of their father's death around the corner, these two are finding the sense to stop the blood flow."

"That and it is bad for business."

The handler put the pen and pad away.

"This is the last meet-up until the feud is over."

"If it ever ends..."

"Well, we can only hope. I have to admit, open gunfire on the streets has made it easier for us to make arrests, but it will never get us close to the snake's head. In addition, we wish to avoid civilian casualties."

They sure have their priorities straight back at the station. I wonder who will get the medal if this ever ends.

"Continue to maintain this momentary peace, agent, and remember. You are nobody without us. If you tell them you're a cop you will face a fate worse than they will ever give you."

"You telling me that doesn't make things any less stressful. I thought you were supposed to help keep my head intact."

"I am because those guys would cave it in with a crowbar, you understand?"

"Yeah, I get it. I want you to help me out though. Find out about the hotel, intel is limited on what happened there, so perhaps you can give me some insight. Here's the address."

"I'll see what I can do, now get out of here."

The handler wandered off while I stayed behind. I removed the manhole I came from and climbed down the ladder. It was a short walk to the next point, but still, it was a sewer. The smell was enough to give me a headache.

Minutes later, I was street-level again and in a different alley. Brushing myself off, I walked back to the pavement and hailed a taxi. It would take me close to the apartment I was staying in, although, after tonight's meeting with the handler, I doubted I would get any sleep. He put more fear into me than Chen.

The old man may have been in his forties, but he still moved fast and carried himself with a sense of power. With that in mind, I was always cautious and confident around him. Weakness or crossing a line meant a quick end. Despite all this, I had grown used to Chen's ways and soon we knew each other well enough to keep the peace.

However, the handler made it more than clear that I was expendable. Everything I did was for them until I messed up, at that point, they didn't know me and I was on my own. More than that, I worried that there was no way out. That I would be stuck protecting a mob boss until I died, which could be pretty soon given the work hazards

I had to continue to play along because I was nobody. The one that had no chance in hell of making it through all this. To be honest, if I was given a way out I wouldn't take it with that girl still living that life. After all, she was innocent and she didn't deserve to be targeted. If it finally came down to it, I would risk my life to make sure Sun Chen never saw her again.

I pushed those thoughts aside as I climbed the stairs of my apartment building. Or should I say, they were pushed aside by an uneasy feeling I had about the hotel? I knew the boss's house, I knew the common meet-up places, but I knew nothing about the hotel.

The other bodyguards told me that it was an old place that belonged to Chen's father, but nothing more than that. I suppose it wasn't too important.

Entering my apartment, I walked straight towards me and fell into the bed. Whatever was going to happen I would handle it. I had to, or as the handler said, I would be seeing my insides.

The Howl

The sound was repetitive, digging deeper into my skull each time I heard it. However, the noise could be allowed if it meant blocking the windows. The wind was howling today, I hated that sound a lot more. When I had finished blocking the sound with the palm of my hands, I picked up a hammer and set to work.

The last window was covered and I returned to my bed. The cold air blocked out and the roaring wind muffled. Massaging the bruises on my leg carefully, I slipped beneath the covers. The pain had yet to fade, but at least I was safe. At least, as safe as I could be in this area.

"Kowalski, are you there? Over." a voice over the ham radio asked.

My eyes drifted towards it along with my hand. Flicking a switch, I then collected the microphone and held it to my mouth. Closing my eyes, I took a breath and answered.

"Kowalski here," I murmured into the microphone. "What's the problem, Trevor? Over."

I released the button and rolled onto my back. There was heat in this place despite the arctic environment. Something we didn't have to worry about losing in our situation. Our heat was sourced from underground volcanoes. On a bad day, you might smell the chemicals.

"The target is two klicks from my station," Trevor began. "From the pattern of its movements, it should reach me in half an hour at least. At that point, it will make a bee-line for you. ETA...uh...two hours. Over."

"Have you tested the machinery?" I asked. "Over."

"I sink just fine, it will pass over no problem. Over."

The target needed the scent of life. Blood of a man or woman would be the most potent and the target would make its way towards the source. Our bunkers were tough, protected from the top mainly. Once the bunker sunk into the ground the scent was masked and the target would head towards the closest scent.

After Trevor, that was me.

We had a limited time below as the descent would cover any leaks to the bunker. This needed to happen to hide our scent. We then raised our bunkers when the creature was close to the next piece of bait in the sequence.

We led this thing around the Arctic in a wide circle until somebody knew what to do with it. However, it has been a little over eight months now and we haven't got any news aside from failed experiments.

"Right, let me know when it's nearing midway. Over and out," I told Trevor.

"Understood. Over and out."

I eased back into the bed and waited for time to pass.

*****

"Kowalski! Kowalski, we have a situation, over," Trevor shouted through the ham radio.

Having not fallen asleep, I was quick to respond.

"What's happened? Over." I asked quickly.

"I have sunk into the ground, but the thing hasn't moved an inch since reaching here, over," Trevor told me in a panic.

I heard a chorus of cursing in my head.

"I heard its howl...I heard it moving, then it stopped," Trevor continued as I was unable to say anything. "Oxygen will run out in forty minutes. I need advice, over."

"Trevor, give it twenty minutes," I told him. "After that, I will go outside and get its attention with a flare. Over."

"Understood, but look at the tracker," Trevor replied. "It isn't moving, not even an inch."

I waited at the radio, preparing warm clothing for the inevitable. It isn't like this hasn't happened before. Usually, it was a pair of other stations that had the problem because the terrain was difficult. The creature would get stuck or it would move too slowly. Still, you were safe as long as you were on the ground.

Twenty minutes passed too fast for me to be happy. I told Trevor that I was going to switch to close communication radio and leave my bunker. He understood and we soon switched to the radios. I placed the device on my jacket and opened the door.

The cold air hit me and my legs were all too ready to buckle. Wavering on the spot, I collected myself and took deep breaths.

"Ahh, God...it has been too long," I told Trevor over the radio. "I forgot how cold it is out here."

"I'm sorry about this," Trevor replied. "I can't help but think that this might be the end for me."

"Let's try and avoid it."

I raised the flare gun and pointed toward the clouds. The trigger was tough for a moment, but once it passed the point of no return, it pulled easily and the flare was shot into the sky. A startling red filled my vision as the bright light ascended. I looked down the line in the direction of Trevor's bunker. The creature was slow-moving without proper motivation, but that flare and my scent would get it moving.

"Trevor, the flare is shot," I told him. "Tell me it's moving."

"I-I...it isn't moving, Kowalski," Trevor told me with a shaking voice. "It's just sitting there, it's in the same spot."

"Trevor, calm down. If it sensed you that well you would hear banging on the ceiling. I need you to confirm if it is there. Reset the tracker and tell me what you see."

"Resetting now, Jason," Trevor murmured.

My first name. It had been a long time since I used it. I was usually the only operative who used first names. Trevor was extraordinarily worried that he finally broke that simple protocol.

"It's still there," Trevor told me. "I'm...I'm raising the bunker. I have to."

"Trevor, if it is there, you fire a flare south and run north, I will see about meeting you halfway."

"I know...wish me luck."

"Good lu-"

In the wind, I heard it. The howl of the black creature. Its silhouette slowly faded into existence as it drew closer.

"Kowalski, there is...there is a hunk of it in the snow," Trevor told me over the radio. "The tracker is in it...it isn't here."

"That's because it's right in front of me," I whispered in reply as the yellow eyes flashed amongst the gray snow and fog.

The hunter had outsmarted its prey.

Keep Going

"Come on, come on, come on!" Lionel yelled as he turned the key.

The car was struggling. Spluttering and grinding itself in response, but no satisfactory answer was given. Eventually, it was fortune that favored Lionel as he smashed his fist against the dashboard, forcing a wire into the right place. The car roared to life.

Lionel wasted no time thanking anyone, he lowered the parking brake and drove down his driveway straight into oncoming traffic. It was thanks to the alertness of both him and the driver that they were able to avoid the collision. With that, the two cars went their separate ways, but it wouldn't be the last car that Lionel nearly hits.

He shook the agitation off and made for the highway. Unlike the few who thought better, Lionel decided to join the majority and race down a long road towards someplace 'safe'.

With safety crossing his mind, Lionel glanced over at his wife in the backseat. She lay there as still as a stone, tied down with a rope and seat belts. Of course, that moment soon passed as his attention returned just before a turn off the side road onto the highway.

"Jason, I hope you found someplace safe," Lionel murmured, thinking of his son now.

Thoughts on his son seemed to slip his mind quickly the more he thought of his wife. Tears rolled from his eyes but were swept away almost instantly as his vision blurred. With emotions clouding him so heavily, endangering him on the busy highway. Lionel clenched his teeth and focused.

With the noises in his head silenced, the night turned from panicked to sinister. Glancing back at his deceased wife in the rear-view mirror, Lionel didn't notice that his wife shifting wasn't entirely thanks to his reckless driving.

Lionel continued to stare at the form before his eyes drifted to the road. Every car was moving at break-neck speeds, which seemed to improve the traffic. Despite there being so many cars, everyone wanted to get there alive as well as quickly.

"Honey?" a voice whispered, barely audible above the engines of the car. However, it only grew louder. "Honey, where are we going?"

Lionel looked up at the rear-view mirror to see his wife sitting up in her seat. The bonds which kept her down were rotted, falling apart like wet tissue. The chair on which she sat was festering at her touch.

"Please, what happened?" the monster asked. "Why are you driving so fast?"

Lionel drew his revolver and pointed it at his wife. Multi-tasking turned difficult as his stress hit its peak/

"Wh-what are you doing?" the creature asked, cowering. "Stop...I...please, don't..."

Lionel pulled the trigger, firing bullet after bullet into the creature until it crumbled with the bonds. Despite having done so already, Lionel felt that the second time should keep it down for good. However, with fear clouding his mind once more and with the powerful distraction, as Lionel fired the last shot a collision occurred.

The car spun and slid across the lanes, only to collide with more cars. Each shock shook Lionel to the point of injury until at last, his car rolled off the road amongst the trees. However, it didn't change the fact that Lionel was damaged now, physically traumatized to go with his mental trauma.

Keep going.

The door of Lionel's car burst open and he stumbled out, grasping wounds as if holding them would fix the bones or lessen the pain. However, as Lionel stumbled, there was a strange crackling behind him. Taking his eyes off the highway, Lionel looked back at his car.

Slowly, a black moss seemed to creep over and take the car over. The door did not open, but the creature crept out of the window, her skin already starting to grow a fungus.

"Lionel? Lionel, are you there?" the creature asked as it writhed. It fell out of the car, hitting the ground at an awkward angle. The neck snapped.

Lionel's heart sank and his skin colour shifted towards deathly pale. Seeing his wife die so many times, yet she kept going...it was breaking him slowly. However, the creature kept going. The neck bobbed on its shoulders, disconnected from the spine in some sense, but held on by the meat and flesh.

"Honey, where are we going?" the creature asked.

"Please, no," Lionel begged, limping towards the highway.

Lionel was on his way, followed slowly by the creature, the space between the two growing. He had fear creeping inside again. How did it get back up so quickly? How does it keep going? However, that didn't matter now, what mattered was defending himself.

Lionel neared a branch on the ground, old and light, but better than nothing. Grabbing it in his strong hand. Lionel swung wildly behind him as he heard the approaching steps speed up. The branch connected, but the force wasn't enough. Turning around, Lionel struck the creature again and again in quick succession. Once it stumbled enough, he took his time with a powerful swing downwards.

The head was caved in, bursting open, spilling black grunge, not blood. The creature, once more, fell to the ground and for good. The body seemed to deflate like a balloon, the blackened grunge spilling out every pore. The skin lay there for a moment longer before dissolving into the dirt.

There was a hiss of heat that soon shifted to a cracking noise as the grunge hardened, then crumbled. His wife, the creature was before Lionel, it became blackened dirt that seemed to rot the living grass around it. Turning from the grisly sight, Lionel walked along the road.

Keep going.

Lionel marched onwards, thumbing for a ride from the many cars until one would stop and take him with them towards the next city.

However, no matter how far he journeys, the creature will follow him everywhere, wearing his wife's skin.

All that Lionel could do when all seemed hopeless and terrifying, was to keep going.

Shiver

When it came to commuting back from the university, nobody was safe. People either lived alone or walked alone. Sometimes both, giving optimal time for a twisted mind to find an opening and take advantage of it. That must have been what happened to me because I believe I was one of the lucky few who made it through alive.

I knew I was alive because I wished I was dead. I woke up in a ditch filled with bodies. Their cold skin sent shivers through me like nothing else, emotionally shaking me as well as physically. The cold was the worst part because it felt like it was stealing my life.

There was blood, but not as much as there should have been. The bodies were pale and had a strange texture. Once I had pulled myself in a panic from the pile, I saw that they had been drained of blood. Slits everywhere, dried blood caking their legs and hands.

With the will to escape, I barely noticed what was around me. My eyes were only drawn to the morbid sight of the body pile. Once free of their grasp, I saw that I was only better off by a small measure.

The surrounding area was hidden in a dense fog, but it was easily broken by dark pine trees, an old farmhouse and barn, and finally a tall mountain in the distance. I never paid attention to the scenery beyond my city, but I took it that I wasn't too far from it. After all, I was assaulted, kidnapped, and drugged, but the more I try to remember, the more I realize that traveling so far was impossible.

I took stock of the mountain and tried to remember if pine trees grew in my state. However, that was information that didn't seem to make itself present despite all my years of learning such meaningless things. I was left standing on hard dirt in the middle of nowhere and I wanted to go home.

My hesitation to head into the fog was great, as I had an ill feeling looking past the dense trunks of pine trees. Something was there, but it was too far, a mere blur from this distance that could have easily been fog or a person. Instead, I chose the next best option, the farmhouse.

I am no fool when it comes to strange places, I've seen enough movies. The barn wouldn't have anything, but the telephone line leading towards the farmhouse was enough to fuel me with the hope of calling for some sort of aid. 'How would they find me?' is the big question.

I spun in the spot, unconsciously checking for more options, but none seemed to present itself. Growing dizzy, I lowered my eyes and noticed that there were similar slits along my hands and feet. However, the blood seemed to have clotted a lot better than the previous victims. I took that as a good sign.

As much as it pained me to consider it, I couldn't go to the farmhouse. The woods may have held some ill intent, but the piles of bodies, and the menacing barn all led me to believe that I was in hostile territory. The last thing that I needed to do was stay here and find out how hostile it could be.

Near the ditch, I saw a pile of clothing. Stumbling towards it, I collected anything to cover myself with. Soon I was comforted by their warmth as the cold air seeped in and made them icy to the touch. However, that was only the first step in the situation and not a particularly great one either. I pushed the thought of these clothes belonging to the others in the ground and marched towards the pine trees.

"God..," I whispered to myself after a moment. "I'm starving."

My stomach panged for some food, but there was none to give. I was hungry and hiking through the countryside. Not my finest moment when I eventually snagged my foot on something I didn't see, but I still felt a lot better the further I was away from the farm.

However, curiosity caused me to look down and examine what had tripped me once I had clambered back to my feet. Laying there in the dirt was a dark iron rod. It protruded from the ground towards a tree but stopped just short of hitting the pine. My mind simply threw it aside like some piece of man-made structure that got lost in the woods a long time ago.

When I reached down to pull at it, however, there was a noticeable click and the woods fell silent. It was so loud, despite the lack of sound. Before I barely noticed the wind, the sound of trees swaying. However, it was now that I realized it was all gone. I lacked any sort of audible sensation, but my sense of touch remained.

It was then that I felt something trickle down my ear. I felt it, then I heard it. The sound of droplets hitting the ground. I thought it was starting to rain, so I proceeded onwards, stopping when I no longer felt the cold water hit me.

"That was quick..." I murmured but stopped myself when something crimson caught my eye.

Something slid down my nose and I quickly wiped it away to reveal it was blood. Red and cold. I felt a sense of uneasiness as I heard the sound of straining ropes above me. The creak of branches as they were bent and pulled by the weight of something on the end of those ropes.

I didn't look up to see what it was. I kept walking, choosing my steps carefully at first. Blinking slowly, I found my heart in this darkness and pushed forward with more enthusiasm. My jog soon turned into a sprint and the trees flashed past me. I would not stay here to learn more about this darkened world. I wouldn't stay to shiver in fear.

My legs began to ache and my constant heavy breathing made my throat sore. However, to stop moving only seemed like a foolish idea in my mind. I collected what fears I had and used them as my energy. It lasted for me until I reached the town outside of the woods.

I saw people on the streets, I saw cars drive by. I left the woods feeling a sense of joy akin to drug-induced euphoria. My grateful desire to be safe was finally fulfilled, so I leaped across the street toward the nearest payphone. Unfortunately, there was not a penny on me, my wallet was missing along with my keys. Even the stranger's jacket I wore was lacking in finances.

I sighed and began approaching people on the street. I saw one turn a corner and I made to follow. I was soon disappointed when I lost sight of them and couldn't find them again. To go further than that, I couldn't find anybody close. Everyone was walking away from me, casually, as if not noticing me there.

I soon realized they did know I was there because when I ran toward them, they ran away from me.

"Hey, excuse me!" I called, running after this one couple wearing suits. "Could I use your phone?"

It may seem like I was the crazy one, but it was them. I soon got close to them, but they just started screaming and running faster. I slowed to a stop and watched as everybody fled. I looked down at my hands. The blood was mostly hidden. I couldn't understand why they were running.

It was then that my eyes glanced toward one of the stores. Perhaps there was a working phone there that I could use and if the owner ran away, all the better. I grit my teeth, groaned through them, and jogged toward the door. I stopped the moment my hand fell on the doorknob.

I could see my reflection in the door's glass pane. I was butchered, my face cut in so many places, red lines leading from my eyes outward. My teeth were painted with blood and my hair was frazzled, hanging in wet clumps from my skull. I screamed and immediately raised my hands to touch my skin.

It didn't hurt physically, but my heart ached to see my face like that. I followed the lines that would become scars on the tip of my finger. I didn't know what was happening to me, but as I did my eyes turned black. I was not the person I saw in the window's reflection and I felt the stress would have snapped my mind if I wasn't distracted.

There was movement on the other side of the door and it opened. A man from the shadows appeared, shadowed by his darkened store, but the barrel of a shotgun, shot forward, hitting my forehead. It hit hard and I fell backward, which was a good thing. I don't think the man intended for me to fall, as the shotgun was fired above me.

If I was still standing, I would be dead, but there was still time for the man to fire again. He pulled the gun to his chest, I heard a click and instinct had me scrambling. I was on my feet and running down the street. Another click. I pictured the man aiming and leaped to the side when I felt it best.

A splattering of deadly pellets hit the ground next to me and I continued running. He couldn't shoot me from this distance and after a quick look back at the store, I saw him shutting the door. He was not going to pursue, but he ensured that I wouldn't return.

"Please, please, get me out of this," I begged the cosmos. "Please legs, don't give in."

I ran past other buildings, afraid that in their now dark rooms, there was somebody as crazy as that man. I didn't even know where I was or what was happening. I was grateful to be alive, but from the look on my face, I wondered how I could still be. After all, it seemed like my face was peeled off and put back.

Not wanting to think about it anymore, or remember my eyes turning black as I touched the lines of my face, I continued to run until I reached the main road. Reading a sign, it pointed to a city I knew of, but it was still far away from home. Ignoring that, the city would be my best option.

I breathed in, focused, and ran. Nobody was following me, that was the good part. The cold, the blood, and the ache in my legs were enough to make the experience painful, but my displeasure had reached its peak. With this in mind, I stuck to the side of the road that was flanked by an open field and not the side flanked by the forest I had left.

I ran and ran, but something kept biting at me. Something that wouldn't let me leave. Coming to a stop, I looked back towards the hostile town. There were people there. Not in town, not right in front of me, but people on the road and field between me and the town.

From the looks of it, they were all regular people. Some were in dresses, some in suits, some casual, some young and even old that were catching up to them. Every one of them stopped and stared at me. I don't know why they were following me, or perhaps they weren't. Perhaps they were just making sure I don't return.

"Leave me alone!" I screamed at them, not helping my sore throat.

I turned and ran. I didn't look back anymore, I was too concerned with staying out of the grasp. Once the main road turned off onto a highway, I gave myself that luxury once more, sure that there were still some normal people in this world that would object to my pursuit.

There was nobody behind me and I was well on my way to the city and getting the help I needed. At least, that's what I thought till my eyes drifted to the forest in the distance. Standing there was a lone man and he watched me with long hair and a dead face. He was closer than the people had been, but far enough that I didn't worry so much.

I walked down the highway and he remained. Watching me till I was just a speck in the distance.

The bus doors hissed and I took the opportunity to leave now. Somehow, I didn't feel safe anywhere. Nowhere felt far enough from the darkened forest, the foreboding mountain. The cold mist seemed to sweep in and out of my life and with it, I felt I saw dark figures watching me within.

Despite there being so many normal people, people cringe with disgust when they see my face but didn't flee or try to kill me. I wasn't as threatened as I was in that town, but I felt that any one of these people could be one of them. These awful people, the ones who must have known what happened to me.

One thing I knew for sure, they never expected me to live through it. Whatever they did to me and all those people in the pit, I was the only one who survived. I wanted to keep it that way, which is why I found myself standing two blocks away from my apartment wondering if I dare return home. After all, that was the last place I remember before waking up covered in the dead.

Did these people abduct me there or on the way from university? I couldn't remember, but I still felt that either way I would be in danger. Instead of returning, I found a phone and used the coins that I begged off the street. It seemed people pitied me more with this face than other beggars. It suited me fine at this moment.

"Mom?" I asked over the phone and she broke down.

I could almost hear the tears. How long have I been gone? It took me three days to get back home, but how long was I missing? I listened to her talk and I got no indication.

"Mom, can you pick me up, I'm at the corner of Smith, by the bakery," I told her impatiently. "I need to see you and Dad. I was kidnapped, but I escaped."

"I will be there in a moment and we can drive to your father," my mother replied but didn't end the call.

She stayed on, explaining how worried she was, and how much she loved me. I heard doors close, I heard a car beep. Next, I heard the rev of the car engine and money began to run out.

"I'm low on change, Mom," I told her. "I will wait for you here."

Hanging up, I took a deep breath and looked all around me. Nobody in sight, nobody that mattered anyway. Beggars sat on the pavement in front of hats, buckets, and cardboard. The sun was setting and my legs were never given a break that meant anything. I decided to sit down near the beggar, huddling with my hood pulled far over my face.

The homeless man glanced at me, catching a hint of my scarred features and his eyes widened.

"Are you alright?" he asked me. A man who was aged by pain asked me if I was alright. It brought tears to my eyes.

"I'm fine...I was just in an accident," I told him. "I..."

I stopped talking, I couldn't. I just sat there and he understood, giving me peace and sitting there with me in silence. I somehow found that more comforting than anything I had experienced so far.

I don't know how long I waited there, but I soon saw a familiar car approaching and driving past me. I stood up with so much hope. Inside I saw the figure of my mother, her eyes darting towards the sign at the corner, looking for me. In the backseat, I saw a strange man, who certainly wasn't my father.

For a moment, I thought it was a new boyfriend, but it was familiar. The two didn't notice me as they drove past, mistaking me for a beggar, but I knew who the man was. He was the one who watched me from the woods. The one who kidnapped me, or at least was a part of the group that kidnapped me. I was starting to believe the latter when I saw my mother in the car with him.

I froze there, wondering what I should do. Pretend I am mistaken and wave them down? I couldn't, I'm not an idiot. I would be crazy to catch the attention of the madman, but my mother was in that car. What should I do?

I decided to watch from afar. I walked across the street and hid amongst the shadow of the building in the setting sun. From the darkness, even my pale face was hidden, giving me a great view of the car stopping and the two climbing out. My mother dashed over to the bakery and looked around.

She soon located the payphone that I was using and neared it, but the man stopped her. She turned to him in fear and talked with him, but he seemed unmoving and silent. He pulled her arm and dragged her back to the car. She complained and at the last moment, she tried to scream.

She was my mother, I stepped forward to make my way there and help her, but I was too late. The man had no fear, no patience. A hand closed over her mouth and wrenched it to the side. The motion was so quick and she was in the car, limp, her head bobbing on the shoulders.

That icy feeling of death so close caused me to stand in place, paralyzed. It wasn't a dead stranger I saw being thrown into the car, not one of the bodies from the pit. That was my mother, she was used and then thrown away as if she were nothing. I fell back into an alley and the car drove away.

I couldn't believe what I had seen. I found a feeling within me when something tapped my shoulder. Turned in fright, ready to fight, but it was only the beggar from before. His miserable face stared at my own and then glanced in the direction of the shrinking car.

"Follow me, I can keep you safe," the beggar told me.

That was not enough for me to trust him and I stepped back. That is when he said something that caused me to stay.

"You are marked, child, they want you dead and you can't hide. I can hide you."

It was nothing and everything. I went with him, not realizing I was saying goodbye to everything.

Fade

How does one approach a snake? I wondered this as my friend, Fox, dug in the sand around the panicked head. A sunburnt prisoner left to rot in the deserts or, as was the case now, be swarmed by the bright green snakes. These beautiful creatures, although small, were a great threat and I stood between one and my friend.

"Shoo!" I yelled at it.

I took a step closer as if to squish it, but it was unmoving. The little snake showed no fear, while I showed plenty in my panicked stance. I always had one foot pointing away from the snake as I was in the squat position. If it were to dart towards me, I would spring away and I believe it knew that.

"Kick sand at it!" Fox ordered as he began to pull the prisoner from the sand.

I did as instructed, shifting my position, standing over the snake, and kicking a bunch of sand toward it. The snake was blocked from sight, but when it settled, the snake was gone. I felt relief for a moment until I felt a tightening around my ankle. Lowering my eyes to my left foot, I saw the small, thin snake had wound itself around my leg.

I screamed in panic, but my left foot remained anchored as I feared that a single movement would set it off and it would bite down on me. However, it was Fox who came to the rescue as a shot was fired. The snake writhed for only a second before falling still. A chunk of it was blown away and the snake unwound in death.

I flicked my foot and sent the snake flying over a dune. I knew that Fox was a great shot, but I counted myself lucky that my foot wasn't blown off. Those guns were unpredictable at best, firing chunks of brass that were razor sharp.

I turned to see the thin, old man lying in the sand with Fox standing over him, loading the gun with more brass shards. The prisoner's face was brown and black, but his skin from the neck down was far paler. The man had experienced hell and it was a miracle that he didn't die or the snakes didn't get to him.

Falling to my knees at his side, I began to attend to the prisoner, giving him water as much as he desired. I rubbed a pale blue cream onto his face and sighed as some skin fell off. I could not hide my disgust and worry from the damaged man. He gazed up at me and his eyes watered.

"You're going to be fine," Fox announced, taking the lead in the treatment. "We just need to get you into a cool bed, my friend."

Immediately, the prisoner was feeling uplifted. He collected himself and even in his weakened state, pushed himself into a sitting position. I could not believe what I was seeing, but Fox had that effect on people. A power to inspire and push them forward. It is why so many followed him, so many strong people became stronger with his leadership.

"Tie him to your horse, we ride now," Fox told me. "The sun shall set soon on this day and we can't let them catch us so far from the fort."

"Will do," I replied, gathering the prisoner in my arms. He was so light.

We saddled up, the prisoner sitting in front of me. He had the strength to hold strong, but I still tied him to my torso so he wouldn't be shaken from the saddle. Fox patted the side of his lean horse. It had the legs for sprinting, perfect for a short distance. However, my horse was built strong for the long haul. I feared that his horse might lag behind and indeed, thirty minutes into the journey, he did.

The night began to fall and stars began to speckle the sky. The prisoner moaned softly, unable to speak, but knowing what this meant. I was the first to spot them after a while and pointed them out to Fox. In the silence of the night, I heard a whisper in the wind. Out of the corner of my eye, I saw a shadow move.

From behind large protruding rocks, their horses appeared, their riders invisible save for the charcoal-black smoke wafting off their invisible riders. The Fading Riders had spotted us and spotted us quickly. It was then I realized the prisoner was bait.

"Fox!" I yelled. "They've spotted us! It's an ambush!"

Fox was already riding between us and them, drawing a pistol, a marvel of engineering. A small gun with many bullets perfect for close range. Fox knew this and it is why he rode to meet the Fading Riders. There was a flash of gunpowder, an explosion of fire as the brass connected with one Rider. More followed, their clawed hands missing with each strike as Fox kept his distance.

However, my attention was soon drawn to the hands of the prisoner which groped at the air around the saddle. I knew what he was looking for and reached down the side, drawing the rifle. I planted it in the prisoner's hands and told him to hold strong. I was immediately caught off guard further when the prisoner aimed the rifle back at me and I moved my head out of the way.

With a deafening bang and a burst of fire behind me, I turned to see a pursuing ghost, who climbed onto my horse silently, and evaporated as the brass destroyed him.

"Thank you," I told the prisoner, although, with my ringing ears, I couldn't be sure if I spoke so clearly.

We soon reached the old fortress, Fox following after us with no pursuers. The gates opened for us and were pushed closed by strong soldiers who watched over them. What followed next was a blur as a mob of people swarmed Fox for orders, panic in their eyes. The prisoner was taken to the infirmary and I followed after the mob.

There always seemed to be something to do and I knew that this would be another long night if the Fade had its way.

Hound

Groundskeeper Alan, a slouching old man from a bygone era, roamed the gardens protecting me from any intruders. Being of noble blood, but living so far from the common people. Thus, I didn't understand why Alan was walking around the manor in the cold, dragging that brutish dog with him.

"Isabelle? What are you doing?" my mother asked from the corner of the room.

I looked over at her shadowy form whose dainty fingers continued to embroider. I focused on the face till it was clear to me, but the features were so aged that shadows played with the face.

"Alan must be cold, Mother," I replied so innocently. It was easy to play innocent at that age, but now it only makes me appear more suspicious. "Why does he have to guard us outside?"

"Isabelle, you know it isn't safe out there," Mother replied. "The common folk are not taken with who we are, thus we are not so taken with them either."

Her words were beyond my understanding, but I got the meaning. It was something I would understand someday, but until then, I was to stay indoors. I never left, just woke up and stared longingly at the outside world. I don't miss those days.

***

"Sounds like hell," Henry murmured, pouring me a glass of wine.

We sat in a busy pub, a pub for all people, not that it mattered to me anymore. I wasn't so noble anymore, just another woman, another commoner. If anything, I felt less than everyone else. I used to have it all, but now I had nothing.

"It was," I replied, taking the glass gingerly from Henry's warm hands. He sat across from me, grunting as he did. "Still, Alan was the one I felt the sorriest for."

"The groundskeeper?" Henry asked.

"So you are listening," I smiled. He placed a hand on mine and smiled too.

"Always, now, what happened to Alan?"

"Alan was always the oldest man there, despite the visits from my grandparents. However, he was a strong man, he served in the first war in his fifties."

"Wow, how did they let him?"

"He was still a military man before he became groundskeeper. There wasn't much opportunity for him anywhere else."

"I see."

"My father was more than happy to hire him, he had a passion for the military, although I feel he would have never made it as a soldier. I think when we all saw Alan pushing himself so hard, in his incredible age, it made us all feel weaker, softer."

"Reminds me of my old man."

"I think almost every family had an Alan. A man too stubborn to let the world beat him down, age or not. He treated his job as groundskeeper seriously and it showed. Everything within the walls was immaculate, not a pebble out of place."

Henry raised his glass to his lips, only to lower it when I fell silent.

"He passed?" Henry asked softly.

***

Mother was sewing this time, but rather sadly. Father had left for work, but she knew better. We all did. There were five of us in that place. A chef, a maid, my mother, me and Alan. We were one maid short thanks to Father, but we were managing. At least physically.

I believe we all felt drained by the miserable season. Rain plagued us, clouds stole the warmth of the sun and the nights were noisy. That day, there were clouds and dense fog. The cold snapped at us, but once every fire was going, the manor warmed up.

I placed my book down, a story of ignorant adventure and I walked to the window. The sight was not a pretty one, but it was made worse with one major difference. There was no old man who patrolled the yard, no old man who made me smile with a cheeky wink and smile.

Alan was missing and I made it clear to everyone. I first told Mother, who ignored me at first, but eventually broke with a sigh,

"Devin!" my mother yelled, calling the chef.

The portly man entered, his hair thin, but mustache thick.

"My lady?" he asked.

"Please, take Isabelle to Alan," my mother ordered.

My mother wished to be alone more than anything. She was even willing to let me walk the grounds with the chef if it gave her some minutes of peace.

I didn't like Devin much, however, that was because I hated the vegetables he served. I was so fussy, so I only made his work difficult. However, he never seemed to mind, he had children just like me. Devin was the one who comforted me that day.

We circled the manor but found no sight of Alan or his dog. Eventually, Devin decided that we should visit Alan's room. A small building separate from the manor, but just as cozy. We were perplexed to see that the chimney didn't have smoke billowing from it. It had to have been cold.

Devin knocked on Alan's door and when there was no response, Devin told me to wait outside while he checked. I waited there for only a minute as something caught my eye at the corner of the house. While Devin searched the house, I approached the show sticking out of a bush.

Alan was dead, torn apart, chewed on, and disfigured. Near him lay his precious dog, with a fat belly and bloody teeth poking from its lips. It slept peacefully until I fell back in horror, crying terribly. The hound woke up, its black eyes focusing on me and with evil intent, it ran towards me.

***

"Devin saved me, killing the dog," I finished. "He was already on his way out of Alan's room and when he heard me, he ran."

Henry sat there, as stoic as stone, pondering darker thoughts.

"Poor man, he didn't deserve such an ending," Henry murmured.

I watched Henry avoid my eyes, finishing his drink. I suppose it was my expression that scared him, perhaps the way I spoke, but the disgust I filled him with was apparent. Nobody understood, but I was really hoping Henry would. I left him in that pub and returned home without a word.

Blue Mirror

"Would you hurry up?" she asked him. "That drill is giving me a headache."

"It can't be helped, we all have our jobs to do," He told her. "Imagine if painting made a noise? Small mercies and all that."

Clarence's wife, Judy, was not in the mood for such talk. The day was going to be a hard one. Moving in is never easy, especially when the house is a piece of work as well. Luckily, the room she was painting was far enough from the hallway that Clarence was drilling in.

Judy entered the office space and closed the door, continuing her painting. There was peace in those moments, while the sun shined through the window, even the birds could be heard chirping. Anybody painting in these conditions would feel pretty relaxed.

After a minute the drill came to a stop, then there was a hammering, but all noise was mostly muffled by the closed door. The only sound that made Judy jump was the shattering noise soon after that. She leaped to the door, pulling it open to see her husband picking up the shards of mirror scattered across the floor.

"The string snapped," Clarence told her, pointing at the limp, aged string hanging off one side of the mirror frame.

"Well, you know what that means," Judy told Clarence with a smile and a shrug.

"Seven years of bad luck?"

"You will have to get the mirror that previous owners left in the attic."

"I'd rather have bad luck, that thing is ugly as hell."

"Well, you should have thought about that when you drilled a hole in the wall and broke the good mirror."

"I smell sabotage."

"Well, you can tell me what the attic smells like in a minute."

Clarence retrieved the heavy mirror from the attic and between the two of them, they were able to get it down the small set of stairs and lug it over to the hall.

"Do you think that bolt can hold this thing?" Judy asked.

"The bolt could hold a car if you balance it right," Clarence answered proudly. "I wonder about this chord here at the back of the mirror."

Slowly the two lifted the large, blue mirror and placed it on the bolt, lowering its weight gently, both ready to catch the mirror if the chord were to snap. However, the chord held strong and the two stepped back to admire their handiwork.

"There, you see?" Judy asked simply. "Was that so hard?"

"What do you think made the reflection so...blue?" Clarence asked, ignoring her smug face. "Is this a hippy mirror or something?"

"It doesn't matter, as long as I have a place to check how I look before work it works for me."

Judy walked away from the mirror and returned to her painting. There were plenty of rooms left to paint, so she sighed deeply and knuckled down. The rooms were empty of all furniture, so she had more fun than expected moving from wall to wall than she did in their bedroom.

Once the last inch was painted she decided to take a break and save the second coat for the next day. Judy opened the door and stopped in her tracks. Ahead of her was Clarence standing in front of the mirror.

"Now, babe, don't develop an ego on me," Judy joked, stepping forward, wiping paint from her hands.

There was no response from her husband, he remained standing there in front of the mirror, staring at his reflection. It wasn't until Judy got closer that she noticed his skin as a mixture of red and blue, veins popping and blood pouring from his nose. Clarence appeared diseased and all Judy could do was scream.

Clarence seemed to react at that moment or perhaps that was the point he finally died. Falling forward, barely missing the mirror, he collided with the wall and crumpled dead on the floor.

Judy stumbled forward, crying in her palms as she stared at his body through her fingers.

"Clarence? Clarence!" she yelled, kneeling beside him, checking his pulse, and pushing him onto his back.

Clarence was ice cold, dead for a long while. It is only for the briefest moments that Judy looked up from her husband, searching for help pointlessly in her empty home, that she glanced at the mirror. It was all that was needed for her mind to pause, an icy grip taking hold of it.

Judy stood up, staring in disbelief at the sight before. In her reflection she saw herself, wearing the face of shock, but beside her stood her husband. He stood smiling and unlike everything else in the reflection he did not have a shade of blue over him. His skin and clothing were their exact colors, but all around him, there was a grim, cool tone.

It was then that Judy noticed her reflection began to grow warmer, the true colors being revealed. At this moment she felt the tightening in her chest as she held her breath. The culprit of the death at her feet was clear so with all her might and willpower she forced herself to look away. In true, physical agony she tore herself from the mirror and took a deep desperate breath in. The coldness of her blood began to fade, warmth returning as her heart returned to its now rapid beats.

The emotions that she embraced drove her to madness, a mind tortured by the will of the mirror, but a mind that had been struck with sudden grief and then purest fear. Judy crawled out the front of her door, feeling as if something was standing behind her now in this house and she had to get away.

Once outside she crawled onto the front lawn and into the sun. The warmth did little to ease her emotions, but it gave her the sense that she was safe now. The grass was green, and the world was vibrant and breathing. However, when she glanced back at the house she saw only her husband closing the door.

A Dark Moon

When I woke up the door was caved in and the room was a mess. Of course, last night's memories had left my mind; I was someone else after all. When I looked around at the mess I saw my torn clothes, the puddles formed by the rain and there was the faint smell of copper in the air. Despite the chains and barricades, my other self had broken free of the cage and I closed my eyes in misery. Even now, despite it being day, I could hear his voice whispering to me. He seemed happy.

I never thought of my other self as 'it', although the newspapers would beg to differ. There was something strangely human about this beast inside of me that I couldn't help but consider as another person. I did everything I could to stop him, but it seems that he is always a step ahead. For now, I was more concerned with the trail I left in the ground leading back to my cage. If someone discovered the result of my actions last night they would be able to track me down effortlessly. However, I was still alive and anonymous, so I took advantage of the time I had.

Fresh clothes and a smart jacket. I shaved and cleaned myself to the best of my ability, removing all evidence and leaving my cage to return to the city. If anything had happened it would help to be at the crime scene and see what the damage was. The last thing I needed to be was a suspect, I know that, but I had a sickening feeling that I should be there.

I climbed into my stowed-away car and drove away from the venue and back into the city. There was always a deep sadness that surrounded the city and its people. The bad circumstance was one thing, but *he* wasn't the only bad person I needed to worry about in the city. As the years passed with this infliction I began to believe I was one of them. I drove for a time and soon stopped outside the TV shop to watch the news which played on the screens. Luckily, there wasn't a crowd surrounding them, which meant whatever I did wasn't as bad as it had been before.

I waited for such a long time, but the politics and disaster that played across the screen had nothing to do with me. What did he do? If he felt as angry as last night I would suspect he would have done something terrible and...big. However, the news that played had nothing to do with him so I started the car and drove home. It wasn't a long way up the city, but the traffic was always a pain. An hour later I was pulling onto my driveway and I saw the flash of police cars. I knew then what he did last night and gathered myself to keep driving in a straight line.

I parked the car by the side of the street, I pushed myself through the crowd and up to the nearest police officer. He saw my movement and marched in front of me and blocked me from crossing the tape.

"Sir, I'm going to have to ask you to stay back," he told me.

I told him it was my home and begged him to let me get inside, but that only made him insist that I stay back more, telling me to give a statement to another officer. I did as he asked and confronted another officer and he asked me for proof of who I am as he began taking down what I said. I searched my pockets but then realized my wallet and identification were with my torn clothes, buried. I explained that I lost my wallet, but in turn, showed him the car keys I had and pressed the remote for my garage door, to prove I live there.

The garage door lifted, revealing the corpse that hung by chains and the police around it taking photos and searching for evidence. I fell to my knees and wept as the office snatched the remote and closed the door to hide the corpse from the view of the civilians who had gasped and screamed in horror. He was upset with me for doing that, but the grief in my eyes was clear and all too familiar to him.

The officers let me cross the line and explained the situation as I wiped my eyes. My wife had been attacked by an animal, most likely a wild dog who was no doubt on the leash of the killer who hanged her in the garage. I wept in response as they continued, telling me no evidence has been retrieved yet, only samples of the animal's hair which

I knew must have belonged to *him*. I asked them what happened to my daughter and they couldn't tell me anything, saying there was no sign of anyone else.

At this, I became hopeful and charged into the house with the police making their way. I made my way into my daughter's room and approached the corner of the room where I had placed a basket over a loose floorboard. I removed the basket and lifted the board to reveal my sleeping daughter. I pulled my baby from the hiding spot and into my arms. I knew that if he ever would come to my home that I should find a better way to keep my family safe other than a few locks.

There was nothing I could have done for my wife without raising suspicion, but stowing my child away on the night was one way to ensure her safety.

The police asked me why I stowed my child away like that to which I found myself struggling to reply. Unable to tell the truth I told them I was paranoid that way. It was why I spent a fortune on the alarm which was destroyed, on the locks that were broken, and the heavy doors that were shattered. My words were easy to see through, but there was no evidence against me.

I knew it wouldn't be the last time I saw the police and I knew it wouldn't be the last time the world saw *him* either. For that reason, I didn't mind them taking away my daughter. I only hoped they would take her someplace where *he* couldn't find her. That way *he* couldn't hurt me anymore.

Scopophobia

There were moments of reprieve. Moments where I was alone in my thoughts, but never when I was asleep. That is when the 'nightmares' gave me a peek inside his mind. The one who wasn't locked inside an asylum. The truly bloodthirsty one. The one who was on his way to claim his next victim and there was nothing I could do to stop him.

I told the nurses that there were times I could talk about it freely, without his watchful eye and keen ears. However, this was usually after he killed someone. It took many years for someone to realize I was predicting newspaper headlines before they happened. The one who realized it was the boyfriend of one of the nurses. A detective was put in charge of tracking down and arresting a serial killer in our cold city.

The time was never right to tell him, but luckily there was a moment where one of the nurses brought him to meet me and my mind was clear before he opened the door.

"He is going to kill again tonight, detective," I told him quickly, jumping from my chair which must have frightened him. I can understand why. I was an asylum patient after all. "He will be in Chester Hotel tonight, his victim is on the third floor, sixth room on the right."

It took some convincing before he said he would look into it, but I had the inkling of a feeling that he believed me after my first warning. It was then that I tried to kill myself.

There was only one way to confirm that he didn't read my mind like I read his. Moving quickly, I pushed the detective back with one hand, the other grabbing the handle of his gun. I noticed it immediately when he entered and the nurse was foolish enough to let him get this far into the asylum with it.

Raising the barrel to my head, cold cylinder pressed against my temple, I pulled the trigger for nothing but a pathetic click. Death did not come and he returned to my mind. He read my thoughts and went quiet as the detective jumped to his feet only to tackle me to the ground.

While he pulled the gun from my hand the nurse clutched his shoulders trying to pull him off me. I put up no fight, there was no point. The killer knew everything now and I whispered as such to the detective. I told him he should have kept his gun loaded and then there would only be one more body in these dark times.

However, I did not get a beating as I expected nor did he write me off as insane. I believe at that moment when he held his hand out to pull me to my feet that I had a friend and I grabbed it, placing my trust in him as I did.

"You can tell that psychopath that if he is listening that he is going to rot in a cell," the detective announced. "My partner, Joseph Lang, knows where he is and is just waiting for the right moment to pull the trigger."

With that warning out of the way, the detective left the room with the nurse and I sat down as the nurse locked the door. I was alone once more with the mental torture that the monster inflicted on me, but this time it was almost bearable. Something about that detective gave me confidence that the killer would be captured. These positive thoughts plagued the killer as much as his bloodthirst plagued mine. I believe in those moments that I was winning.

A few days passed before it happened. I felt a sense of relief that I never had before. I felt quiet, a peace that was lasting longer than a few moments. The monster was gone and I knew it. At last, I was free of the horror, he was dead.

The nurse returned to check on me an hour after this to find me dancing in the room, overjoyed. She stopped at the entrance and watched me with a smile. As I had my back turned at that moment, it all returned with a fury. I felt the suffering hit me like a stone and tears were in my eyes.

In those moments I could see what he saw and I saw me. I turned back to the nurse to find her studying me coldly, my mind in agony at this sudden realization.

"It...it's you?" I asked her. She nodded in reply, closing the door. "But how...how did you stop the thoughts?"

There was no reply from her, but it didn't take much for me to realize that she had been playing me and the detective all along. There was madness within her that was beyond my understanding and she was using that ignorance against me.

I would have felt that my days had come to an end if I still didn't hold that shred of hope. Once that was all I had and the cold blade of a knife pressed against my throat, I heard it. A shocking silence and blood poured.

Her hand went limp, the blade falling to the floor with her after it. With the killer dead, I saw in the doorway a mournful detective who fell to his knees. He knew in those moments that he did the right thing, but there was something between those two that made him deeply regret his actions.

I pushed myself up into a sitting position, staring down at the body. Blood ran down her forehead from where the bullet left her skull, her face painted with shock. She was my sister, but the bane of my existence. With all the watching, I could not see what was right in front of me.

I didn't feel the same sadness as the detective and in time he didn't either. What died that night wasn't a woman, a normal human. It was a cold-blooded monster who met a suitable end. With that thought, the detective and I shared a similar peace.

Unknown

"Sign here," the lieutenant told me. I didn't see why I should be in an operation such as this, after all, we aren't supposed to be there. It then dawned on me that it was a test, so I shook my head. "Good, follow your commanding officer to your station. Your team of scientists will be waiting for you and you are to protect them at all costs. Further details as to why will be with them. Good luck, soldier."

He saluted me grimly and I followed suit before leaving the small building and walking with Officer Lion, a name he adopted for these ghost operations.

"You are to be equipped with a standard assault rifle and a handgun," Lion explained, "You will be stripped of all identification documents and tags, that includes your dog tags. Don't worry, if you don't return your family will be informed, so there is no need to go out there and get you, is that clear?"

"Sir, yes, sir," I replied, but my voice had lost all major confidence. Still, I maintained professionalism and gave the situation my best game face.

We arrived at a small tent where there were plain-clothes men with glasses. One was short and chubby and the other was trying to brush the mud off his boots. I looked at Lion and he rolled his eyes. Our feelings were mutual on dragging these two through the jungle, but we kept it to ourselves. At least for now.

"Tell me there aren't snakes in this place?" the short one asked.

"There are snakes, doc," Lion replied as he gestured for them to follow. I collected my guns on the table and marched with them.

"Oh, I'm not a doctor. I am an expert in the field."

"Shouldn't an expert have a doctorate?"

"This field isn't taught in universities, officer."

"Right..."

It was getting on into the night and so far we didn't hear any complaints from the scientists as we left camp. Officer Lion had the official coordinates to the site, memorized of course. The scientists were the only ones with any recording equipment. We made no mistake in their value to the government and what they didn't seem to understand was that they outranked us in respect to our superiors.

Officer Lion respected authority, but I could see how he was struggling to find respect for these two. The stick figure danced between bushes and always seemed to be keeping himself from falling over. The short one had already worked up a sweat that drenched his shirt.

Soon we entered the edge of the jungle and from there Lion began enforcing a rule of silence.

"You two are to remain silent," Lion explained. "Not only are there snakes, but other predators will more than likely like to sink their teeth in you."

"And assault rifles are how you are going to deal with them?" the stumbling one asked.

Officer Lion didn't respond, but like me, he knew well enough that nothing could be ruled out in this operation. Even the ammunition we were using was specially made to avoid any affiliation with the US. I think if they didn't realize it then, the scientists soon realized that if push came to shove they would be terminated on the spot.

If they did realize it, they sure had a pair for acting so confident throughout this experience.

"Ryan, are you seeing this?" the tall one asked. I rolled my eyes, they were already breaking protocol by using their real names.

"I see it, but keep your system ready for spotting the signatures, not hearing them," the short one replied. "It is great having the recordings, but we need some footage."

"Don't worry, I am."

We were nearing an hour in the jungle, Lion was silent the whole way. It made me tense, the silence. Officer Lion was listening, but not hearing what he wanted to hear, but we soon arrived.

Entering a small patch of darkened clearing, the scientists saw what we found a week before. The grass was black, coated with what appeared to be oil, and above us was a machine so foreign it couldn't be identified by Russian and Asian forces.

It would be shipped back to an American facility where the world's specialists could study it, but until it was moved the landscape needed to be examined. The scientists picked their jaws up and all fear of mud and snakes vanished. The two fell to their knees and began setting up their many devices.

"It isn't toxic, but the structure of the liquid is..." the tall one murmured, trailing off into jargon.

"It could be a mixture of carbon-based fuel, but that is..." the chubby one replied with a string of his science.

I turned to Lion as the scientists had their mini field day. He seemed to be watching the treetops, but I found my attention was drawn more to the shadows in the forest. As dark as it was, there seemed to be plenty of areas that were void of any light. It would have been perfect for someone to watch us from. It was these areas that made us expendable.

Twenty minutes later and our patience was finished.

"Pack your stuff up, we're leaving now," I told them. Lion pulled them up after they grabbed their tech.

We marched them in the opposite direction of the site, but my eyes were watching that area closely. My rifle was raised and the safety off.

"Jeez, we were just getting some great data," the short one complained.

"You had your twenty minutes, now shut up," Lion grunted.

"Lion, I see movement," I murmured as a shadow crossed from one bush to another, definitely humanoid.

"We are a thirty-minute run from base camp, this is not the time to be fast. Silence, now."

All four of us fell silent and continued our walk back to base. As we neared the edge we picked up the pace and left the jungle. Returning to base our tension was slowly eased. At least until we found them all. Every soldier and officer was in a pool of their blood.

"We need to evacuate," I told Lion. "The facility is compromised and then some."

Lion nodded in agreement, his eyes narrowed. A face I had seen on many soldiers, unfortunately, it was usually the scared ones. I could only hope that Lion was as confident as he looked. All four of us marched onwards, the scientists finally silent, as Lion and I were the only ones left that separated them and the world's greatest threat.

Reaching the helipad, we were all disappointed to find more bodies and no helicopter. The jungle seemed to move all around, our stalkers surrounding us.

"Everyone died here and we didn't hear a thing," I told Lion. "Let us not go out so quietly."

We raised our guns and pointed them at the jungle's edge, only to be surprised by the sound of a helicopter, which dove toward us. It was going to do a quick landing, I could tell that much. Yet, I took my eyes off the jungle for too long. I saw claws, a figure, and eyes...more eyes than there should be.

I fired my rifle, blinding flashes and a kick that took a moment to control. I saw blood, my own, and then waking up here, somehow alive, but not in one piece. It is a threat that cannot be handled by the ground troops. If you want my advice, if you want to save the human race, you need the scorched-earth mentality.

And then some.

The Anomaly in Skates

Jackson threw his apron into the laundry bin in the staff room. Another day at the restaurant was wasted on the same four customers and a new guy who just wanted to use the bathroom. With each day he wondered if he should find a new job before the place closed down, but his boss was always enthusiastic about there being a change. Yet, Jackson knew the change that would happen wouldn't be for the better.

"I'm going home!" Jackson yelled as he walked out the back door.

"Right, see you tomorrow!" his boss called back.

Jackson wandered back to the front of the restaurant and began his walk home. He lived in a quiet neighborhood, a simple one. It really shouldn't have surprised him that the most customers he would get would be regulars or travelers passing through town, but he still wished to cook more than the same stack of pancakes and steak dinner every day.

These niggling thoughts bothered him all the way up the block until they were disturbed by the sound of a trash can falling over. The metallic sound of it hit the ground up the road from him and the can began to roll down the road. Jackson watched it pass him with a struggling raccoon inside.

Jackson would have laughed if he didn't walk into someone.

"Oh, I'm sorry," Jackson replied, catching the stumbling person. "I didn't see you there."

Jackson kept the woman from falling over and she smiled as her feet wobbled. She was wearing skates and for a brief moment, Jackson wondered why he didn't hear her as well.

"Don't worry about it, can you give me a push?" she asked.

"I'm sorry?"

"Can you push me down the sidewalk, I have trouble getting some momentum."

"Uh...sure."

Jackson walked behind her as she positioned herself to face down the pavement he walked and he pushed her lower back. With that, she began skating away and gave him the thumbs up as she disappeared around the corner.

Scratching his head, Jackson returned to his walk up the road. After a moment the distractions lost their effect and he pondered once more on finding better work. Perhaps moving to the city like his father always suggested, but something in him showed no interest in leaving the small town.

Fingers gripped Jackson's shoulder and he turned in surprise to see a tall man. He was elderly and bony, skin seemingly hanging in bags off his head. The stranger wore dark gloves, a trenchcoat, and a formal hat. Jackson's eyebrows raised at the sight of the grim-looking man.

"Can I help you, sir?" Jackson asked.

"I am looking for my granddaughter," he informed Jackson. "Have you seen her?"

"Uh...I only saw a girl with roller skates."

"That is her. Do you know where she went?"

"I don't know, down that way I think," Jackson replied, pointing the old man back down the road.

"Thank you," the old man nodded and was about to release his shoulder and leave, but he hesitated, looking back at Jackson. "You didn't touch her, did you?"

The question was asked aggressively and Jackson suddenly felt incredibly intimidated.

"Uh...no," Jackson lied. "Of course not."

"Good."

With that, the man marched off down the road, and this time Jackson paused. Was it right for him to point the stranger in the right direction? After all, he was the right age and he seemed harmless despite his stature. Still, when the elderly man turned the corner, Jackson couldn't help but fear the worst.

With a sigh, he decided to walk after the old man. If anything was off he would intervene, but even then he wasn't sure how. Perhaps he should call the police if something does go bad, but that would take far too long.

The more Jackson thought the more he felt there was no real danger. The woman didn't seem like she was running away or anything and that old man could have been overly protective. Jackson saw him turn the same corner as the girl and when the old man was out of sight his worries grew.

Jackson jogged up the road and approached the corner to hear a strange sound. It was a curious sound, but it seemed oddly familiar. He hesitated to turn the corner, so he leaned forward and peaked to see where it was coming from.

The old man was laying on the pavement, face down, while the woman from earlier stabbed his back with a kitchen knife. Each plunging strike sank deep into the back of the old man. The next strikes were playfully done by the woman who seemed to be enjoying herself.

Jackson's eyes widened and the only thought on his mind was escape. He chose his steps carefully, making sure his steps didn't make too much noise as he made his way up the pavement. The stabbing sound, which he found familiar to his work in the kitchen, faded slowly but never ceased.

"Oh...God..." Jackson began to whisper to himself as he made his way up the road.

He could no longer hear the stabbing noise and decided it was time to run. He leaned forward, raising his knees as he broke off into a straight sprint away from the scene, but began to slow down immensely when he saw what was ahead of him.

It was the same woman, struggling on her roller skates, down the pavement. She couldn't have gone so far ahead of him, but there was no doubt it was her. She wheeled past Jackson and into the fence of the house he was in front of. She turned to look at him.

"Hey, can you give me a push?" she asked. "I have trouble getting up to speed."

Jackson stared at her, his mind burning, he had almost forgotten what happened, but the memories clung on. Despite all the mental conflict, Jackson helped...again, wondering what was happening.

"S-sure," he murmured, wondering if he was going insane.

Hesitantly and ever so carefully, he pushed her lower back once more and she was propelled down the pavement, giving him the same thumbs up.

Jackson watched her turn the same corner and he began to run home once more. Soon after, he saw the familiar sight of the old man who held up his hands to stop Jackson. The old man could see the panic in Jackson's eyes.

"You touched her, didn't you?"

Surreal

There are those days when the world seems to turn so strange. I find myself grasping at straws as if they were sticks of reality. I find the world splintering, then melting then in a panicked blink everything is as it was and nothing changed except me who revealed his madness to the world. I felt their eyes on me as I struggled to maintain myself, to preserve my life in these strange experiences. I would leave and try to avoid these people, but I soon realized there would always be people like that.

I also spent too much of my youth running in fear or cowering as the world broke down around me. There was so much that could go wrong if I panicked, so I decided around my teens to accept what the world was to me and watch as it all disappeared and reappeared.

I remember the first day I tried this method. I was in class watching a science lesson show me what molecules did in their different states and then I watched as everything began to vibrate. I suppose the lesson had a great effect on me as I began to see the world as if it were vibrating molecules. Watching those tight clusters of atoms called people and objects, but also watching those molecules that would be a lot less static as millions of atoms would fly from the object and bounce around this world at a great distance.

It was safe to say that lesson had the greatest effect on me when I realized that the atoms of everything could either be static like the objects we saw them or as frantic as beams of light. It was wholly strange to realize that I shared the atoms of everyone in that room and scientifically speaking, we were all of the same entity. By the end of that, I took it further and followed the bouncing atoms of the universe and realized that we were all one cosmic being that would never die and our planet was much an atom to the rest of the universe, everlasting, but everchanging and insignificant.

By the time the lesson ended, so did my hallucination and I left the class smiling. It was odd in itself, but then again, everyone seemed happy to leave the class. My experiment with these hallucinations went further to the point of my first job.

I had been working there for nearly three months and doing well. I even believed that promotion was on the way because some higher-ups retired or were simply let go. It left openings that needed to be filled by the most qualified employee and that was me.

Of course, that changed when I had another hallucination in the middle of my work. These things never lasted for long and I figured I could continue with my work just ignoring them. However, everything was altered when I was in that surreal trance. My vision, my hearing, and even my sense of touch. So when it came down to writing a list of instructions to newer employees I had used a metal ruler to carve the list into an unrelated book.

The pages tore of course and soon people noticed. When my hallucination ended it was downhill from there. The fear in their eyes when they looked at me was heartbreaking. I had known these people so long, some even from university and they knew about my disorder. Still, so many of them could only imagine it as if there was a knife in my hand and a person I was cutting the list into. It would never happen, nowhere near possible, yet some just spread their fear and any consideration I had of being promoted was dashed in a moment.

I returned home that day saddened, rather than angry. There was so much wrong with what I saw, but it was affecting my life harshly. I used to get by and accepting my hallucinations only took me to higher places. Now, it was a hindrance and my mind began to work against me.

Negativity pushed some special buttons and the hallucinations became much more frequent. From having one a week to several in a day. It was my worst nightmare brought to life and that disturbing feeling only made it worse. What could I do to fight it? Nothing, but be still.

Now, there were times when it would be bad to stay still. Crossing the road for instance or leaving a train at your stop. You can tell where I am going with this. I was starting to arrive late to work and even when I was there I wasn't getting much done. My mind wouldn't let me.

I was fired for not completing my tasks and yes, I could have sued them for firing me over my disorder, but I promised them it wouldn't happen. I could understand their feelings and quite frankly, they were my friends up till the end. I was given a sad farewell and driven home and guided into my apartment. I was given calls now and then from the people at my old work to check and see if I was doing okay.

When my moments passed and I saw the apartment, the madness of objects it had become. The clutter, the hoarding, the horror. I lied to them and told them everything was alright.

I was stuck, stuck in a situation I could not accept and would not accept. I had no money, no job and I was fast losing hope. I turned to the only people that had my back through thick and thin although we didn't part on the best of terms. I called my parents and they arrived to save me. My apartment was cleaned, and the trash was moved from the building as I was too scared of wandering into traffic.

I love them more than anything, but to help me despite the conflict we had in the past...that was something I could never pay them back, even though I tried to every day after that. Now, it was all a matter of finding out how to live in these conditions.

Sitting at a desk wasn't something I enjoyed, I preferred to be outdoors. It was one of those painful things I needed to accept with my condition. The less time I spent outside, the better. There was no safety and with eyes playing tricks on me, it was a death wish as well. Thus, I sit at a desk, feeling the keys of a keyboard and opening my heart to the world.

There would still be times that I worried about my safety. For example, opening the door to the bathroom. I would pause there for the longest time and wait for the hallucination to end before I braved stepping onto the cold tile. As you can imagine, spending two hours or so a day doing nothing but making sure everything was real was only a waste of time.

Even after all my family did for me and the fact I was getting some sanity back, I still felt hopeless. The apartment was cold and empty, the words I expressed were only getting darker and inching towards misery. I could feel collapse, I could hear cracks in the building and I was all too ready to accept doom and destruction. I was close to giving up.

That is when I met her. A strange individual trying to open her apartment door across from mine. I was taking out the trash, as carefully as I could. I had given myself a good forty minutes to complete this with the threat of walking into the road or off an edge towards a fall. When I opened the door, I saw she was trying her apartment key, but it wasn't happening. With a final burst of frustration, the key snapped and she yelled.

I jumped in surprise and she heard. When she turned around I saw a whirlwind of chaos. A mess of tangled hair, glasses that kept falling off her small nose, hands filled with notepads, and a satchel. On top of that, even the scarf she wore seemed to be against her. It was longer than any scarf I had ever seen and it seemed to wrap around her like a boa constrictor.

"Uh," was all I could say, blinking too much for her to think I was sane, but she didn't seem to notice.

"Oh, can I use your phone, please?" she panicked. "I need to call the super to get this door open."

I didn't think to question her, but I saw an opportunity to shorten my forty-minute venture to ten at the most.

"Sure, go ahead," I replied, pushing the door open and pointing at the phone which clung to the wall.

It was only when she passed me that I realized she could have been trying to break into the apartment across from me and now I just gave her an apartment to rob. However, on looking at her again as she dialed the number, she didn't seem the type.

A minute later she walked out.

"Thanks, he will be here in a few minutes," she told me. "I'm Eliza, by the way."

Instead of a handshake, I got a small wave and a smile.

"Chester," I replied with a nervous nod. "Cou-could you walk with me, Eliza? I need to take this..."

I didn't need to finish, she just nodded.

"Sure, lead the way," Eliza murmured.

She began to take her phone out, which worried me if she was going to watch me from making a mistake. However, Eliza simply took it out to turn it off. With a sense of relief, I began walking down the stairs and discovered a trait about Eliza. She was a talker.

"What a day, huh?" Eliza began simply enough before a torrent of peeves flew from her mouth. "The moment I stepped out of work a car decided to speed through a water puddle right at my feet."

Looking at her closer I did notice some water still clinging to her hair.

"And this scarf, ugh, my mother knitted it, but to fit her! She is like seven-foot compared to me! I'm trying to help this one lady find a book and I just keep tripping over this giraffe attire."

I made a small laugh, although nervously as we were now outside. Walking behind the building to the dumpster I paused as the alley disappeared. I was in complete darkness now and my step didn't seem to find solid ground. I stopped moving at this point, knowing that if I couldn't feel the ground I should pause completely. It would be so easy for me to fall over.

I felt it then. A presence. It wasn't malicious, but it seemed to be watching me closely. I wondered if it was for its amusement, to see me suffer. It was speaking to me, telling me to do something. I don't know what exactly, but I seemed to be further away from the dumpster than before.

"And what do you do, Chester?" Eliza asked me.

"Uh...can you hang on a second?" I asked her, but I must have been failing in keeping still.

Eliza grabbed my arm.

"Are you alright?" Eliza asked, more concerned than I expected from a stranger.

Eliza guided me to the dumpster as I explained what was wrong with me. She even guided me back up the stairs and the moment I felt my apartment door handle I pushed it open I heard another voice, luckily this one was real.

"What can I help you with?" I heard his gruff, old voice ask.

"I will be okay, thank you, Eliza," I told her as she lingered back and I closed the door.

With the door closed, I dropped on all fours, but it felt like I was floating through space. I lay there for around twenty minutes before I blinked the right blink and the world returned. I sighed deeply before standing up and returning to my desk to write some more.

However, as I was sitting down there was a knock at my door. To my surprise and relief, it was Eliza.

"All sorted?" I asked, playing it off as if nothing happened.

"Uh, yeah, I'm back in," Eliza replied, but I saw the same concern and fear in her eyes as everyone else. "Are you...alright?"

"Yeah, don't worry. Thanks for keeping me from face-planting into the sidewalk."

"Hey, no problem," she replied a little more chipper.

I nodded awkwardly and was about to close the door.

"Uh, Chester, do you want to hang out and, like, talk some more?" Eliza asked. "Believe me, talking does help. You heard it from me firsthand."

"I don't-" I began, but was almost instantly interrupted.

"I'm not taking 'no' for an answer," Eliza replied simply. "Come on, I made coffee."

I believe with those words I was sold and ever since the world was a lot quieter.

Do You See?

"Okay, Jackson, we are going to increase the flow of the chemical," Doctor Hart spoke into the speaker.

"Understood, Doctor," Jackson replied from inside the chamber. It was cold and the chair he was strapped to was far from comfortable. He could feel his heart beating faster in the excitement and fear. "Perhaps do it in a small increment this time, any more of this stuff and I won't wake up."

"I know what I am doing, Jackson, but I will lessen the increase a little if you are unsure."

Hart pushed a button once the levels had been set and an inky liquid ran through a tube into Jackson's neck. He could feel the cold liquid enter his body. His warm blood couldn't keep the goosebumps from appearing all over his body and his stable mind couldn't stop the headache that followed. Still, the dark empty chamber that he sat in didn't have anyone else but him.

Both Hart and Jackson gave it time to set in, but Jackson was fast losing hope in the idea that they would ever see the creature again. Perhaps that time was different, but they were recreating the circumstances perfectly, increasing the dosage of the chemical if it helped. Jackson was about to shake his head to conclude the experiment, but then he felt the overwhelming sense that he was being watched and looked up.

Staring down at Jackson was the black snout of the creature, beady eyes above its nose, while the rest of it hung in shadow. Perhaps it was there the whole time, but Jackson doubted it.

"Okay, Hart, it's here and right above me," Jackson replied with a growing sense of fear.

"Right, okay...uh..." Hart replied, trying not to panic. "What can you observe from its behavior?"

"It appears to be observing me, Hart. Black eyes, black nose, but the rest I can barely see. I don't think it likes the light...perhaps-"

"We are not turning the light off, Jackson. We haven't confirmed if it is afraid of the light yet or if it is hostile. You know this."

"It didn't attack before, I don't think it will now. It doesn't seem to be breathing...at all."

Doctor Hart pondered this. The creatures have been known to be seen if enough of the chemical entered the body of the observer, but once more, Hart also believed that the creatures need to want to be seen in addition to the chemical. These creatures were intelligent, therefore, not to be trusted.

"No breathing? Do you hear anything? Smell anything?"

"Nothing...oh god...Hart, there isn't a smell of it at all."

Hart immediately slammed his fist over the emergency button and two halves of a capsule began to close around Jackson. The creature sensed it and immediately the lights cut. The last thing Hart saw before darkness filled the chamber was the creature fluttering into the capsule before it closed. Jackson began screaming and he didn't stop.

"Alpha Team, move in, flashlights and torches readied!" Hart yelled into a separate microphone.

The doors to the chamber opened and the four soldiers moved in, lighting the chamber up with the brightest lights they had in possession. Hart opened the capsule and there was just a writhing mass. It took a moment for Hart to realize the screaming had stopped. There was only the sickening noise of biting and chewing. The lights did the trick and the creature began to smoke and disintegrate, but that didn't stop the soldiers from speeding the process alone with high-intensity light bursts from the rifles.

The creature didn't make a sound as it broke up into nothing, revealing the scratched and torn body of Jackson in his chair. Hart bit back his anger and sadness. The creatures were smart, but not smart enough to know that the friendly creatures seemed to have a peculiar smell, a small sign that is often forgotten. Doctor Hart sighed and ended the recording to return to his office. The alpha team left the chamber, closing the door behind them

The report was filed and sent to everyone in the facility informing them of the news.

Most likely, everyone was just used to death. The world was now draped in perpetual darkness, the windows covered with armored shutters, ensuring no light escaped. Not to mention, every room was constantly lit, further ensuring if a hostile creature made it inside that it would suffer. A life of living in the light was an uncomfortable one, but it was better than being attacked by those creatures.

Hart entered his bright office and sat at the desk, closing his eyes to ease the pain. The chemical that was pumped into Jackson's body was the cold blood of one of those creatures. If enough of it was stored in the body it made creatures more comfortable around humans, as if there was another creature in the room. However, it didn't protect a human once the creature saw it wasn't one of them. Jackson knew these risks but was still happy to be a focal part of the experiment.

"Doctor Hart?" Betty asked from the door to his office.

"Yes, Doctor Goldberg?" Hart muttered.

"There has been discussion circulating this facility that...haven't exactly been positive towards our goal," Betty replied cautiously. "With the loss of Jackson, I need to know if these rumors are true."

"And if they are, would you want to know?" Hart asked, standing up. "Or would you want to hang onto the hope that whoever is still alive in this world has a chance to be rid of these creatures or hidden from them?"

Betty was silent and staring at her feet, unable to decide on an answer.

"Goldberg, go back to your lab," Hart ordered. "These rumors you are hearing belong to the people who have given up. The people hate us because we are using so many resources in the pursuit of a solution.

These people are wanting a faster solution to our troubles, but the only solution like that for them is to put themselves to sleep. It saddens me that these are the people I am trying to save, but in the end, I became a scientist to help people beat these problems. I suggest you use your free thinking to ponder why you became one as well."

With that, he closed the door to his office so that he may be left alone to his work.

Despite Hart's speech, deep down. he wondered if it would be better just to leave it all behind, abandon everyone and take what he needed to survive comfortably on his own. As the lights in his office and the rest of the facility, he realized someone else had made such a decision already.

Thank You for Reading!

More stories are always on the way! Thank you for taking the time to read through my second collection of stories, I truly appreciate my readers and my supporters.

Be sure to check out my channel, The AURORA Files, there's always more content coming out. If you are interested in reading the next collection of stories, be sure to have a look at my Patreon page.

As always, I am always working to make my next stories that much more scary.

I wish you all the best and thank you for reading!
Matthew Dewey

tfepe wgjj amke s rsy wfel tfglbq spe st tfegp wmpqt wfel gt deejq jgie
lmtfglb gq wmpiglb mut wfel jmve dsgjq ymu slr elekgeq wgjj ksie
kmpe qelqe tfsl dpgelrq desp wgjj pesaf gtq nesi cut gt wgjj lmt ce
elmubf pekekcep wfm ymu spe wfm fsq sjwsyq ceel tfepe dmp ymu slr
nut mle dmmt gl dpmlt md tfe mtfep tfe evgj wgjj nsqq slr ymup fespt
wgjj tfsli ymu dmp lmt jgqtelglb tm gtq nslgaier wmprq

Also by Matthew Dewey

Dread
Dread: Volume 1
Dread: Volume 2
Dread: Volume 3
Dread: Volume 4

Shadows
Shadows of Dread: A Collection of Sinister Stories
Shadows of the Unknown: A Second Collection of Sinister Stories

Standalone
Writing Better Main Characters
The Fantasy Writer's Handbook: A Comprehensive Guide for
Beginners